Advance pr[...]

"Witty, hilarious, moving—a wild romp through the luminous landscape of the Pacific Northwest where mountains appear to float in air and the line between reality and fiction blurs. An original first novel that made me think of Nabokov on speed."

> —Mary Elsie Robertson, author of *What I Have to Tell You*

"Audacious and irresistible, *Sedimental Journey* is truly a trip. Widerkehr has conjured enormously appealing characters from off-the-wall Alton to scratchy-voiced Eloise. Setting [his tale] in a small town with a university geology department as backdrop, Widerkehr deftly exposes the hidden layers of his characters' lives. A quirky novel the reader will not soon forget."

> —Margot Rowe, author of *Facade*

About *Disappearances*:

"The language of *Disappearances* is fresh and musical, the observations of nature precise and surprising. These are poems to savor…Widerkehr's world, where a tender attentive regard meets what John Updike calls the 'jittery spirit' of self-consciousness."

> —Jay Klokker, author of *In Bear Country*

To Donna,

Hope you enjoy this.

— Richard
4/17/04

Sedimental Journey

"It is not down on any map; true places never are."

—Herman Melville, *Moby Dick*

Also by the author:

Disappearances
(a poetry collection)

sedimental Journey

Richard Widerkehr

Richard Widerkehr

Tarragon
Books

Cover design by Karen Parker

This is a work of fiction. Names, characters, places, and
incidents either are the product of the author's imagination or
are used fictionally, and any resemblance to any actual
persons, living or dead, events, or locales, is entirely
coincidental.

ISBN: 0-9724986-0-5

Library of Congress Control Number: 2003114132

10 9 8 7 6 5 4 3 2 1

Tarragon Books
1424 E. Maplewood Ave.
Bellingham, WA 98225
www.TarragonBooks.com

For Linda,
and for my mother and father.

I did not write this novel quickly, so I have many people to thank for their encouragement and suggestions:

Lynda Schor, Kelly Cherry, Jim Rogers, William Wiser, Mary Elsie Robertson, Richard and Roz Spitzer, Margot Rowe, Bob Cloud, Jody O'Connell, Barbara Diamond Goldin, Mitch McCarrell, Jay Klokker, Chris Suczek, Craig Leslie, and Sara Stamey.

I especially want to thank Linda Ford and my parents, Andy and Mary Widerkehr, for their steadfast love.

ONE

Once I was a reasonable man. That was before the trial separations, before I fell in love with a fictional character, a woman in a book of short stories. Facts are facts, and I believe in stating them. My father, a reasonable man, says, "Crying gets you nowhere," and he's right. That's where it got me. Nowhere.

Facts made me Alton Broome, assistant professor of geology at North Cascades University. As a rule, geologists don't make a big deal out of the soap opera side of life. They take the point of view of the millennia, the ages, the Grand Canyon's point of view. They take separations in stride. They don't fall for fictional characters. Eloise Hartwig is—or was—fictional.

But first came the six trial separations. Each time Clarissa and I broke up, we said tearful goodbyes in the basement of the bank where we kept our joint account. Six times we took off our wedding rings and laid them in our safe deposit box, in case we changed our minds. Six times we stood by the clanking iron door, signing and countersigning forms. Soon a judge would likely parcel out our house and cars, my rock collection and Clarissa's antique jewelry collection. Luckily, we are childless.

As a child, I wasn't always as reasonable as my father, Boomer Broome, could have wished. When he lounged in the TV room, watching *Bat Masterson*, reading *The Wall Street Journal*, chainsmoking Lucky Strikes, eating raw onions, and farting, sometimes I'd ask, "Daddy, don't you think Bat Masterson is stuck-up?"

"What do you mean, stuck-up? Define your terms." He glowered, smoky as Vesuvius on a bad day. "What's wrong with being proud? Reasonable men are proud. I might add that you, Alton, would be a more reasonable child if you didn't mumble when defining terms. Speak up."

✠

The day I heard from Eloise—and her creator, Emily Weed—hadn't been one of my better days. Clarissa and I had met in cubicle number three at Cascadia Commercial, where we never did as well as we did in number one. In fact, she took off her white-gold ring, closed my fingers on it, and tugged my fist in front of my nose. She left, and I deposited our rings myself.

It was after four-thirty when I walked out onto Commercial Street. The ornamental star on top of the Mount Baker Theater's white turret sparkled in the twilight. It had been raining for a month—since October—the way it does in northwest Washington. The sky, black at the horizon, had a bulging, gray overhang above. Past the brick tanks of the pulp mill, logs like old bones lay beside heaps of sawdust.

I kept seeing bits of a dream I'd had the last two nights in a row. My students from the last sixteen years made a worm of a line winding into the Grand Canyon. There was Gracci, who argued about his grade ten years ago. I gave him an A because I didn't want him to think I was vindictive, and he had improved. There was Brill who always got A's, she told me in a firm, injured tone, and whom I'd been just as firm with. There was Noll, who answered a ten-point question on geological time with a touching essay on "the necessary steps necessitated to make something of yourself." There were students I'd had crushes on—Miss Spreck, Miss John, Miss Stringer, and Miss Van Sand—none of whom I'd spoken with outside of class.

In my dream, my favorite students flew past the Coconino Sandstone and the Bright Angel Shale, tumbling toward the black, Precambrian layers at the bottom. "Hooray!" each one yelled as he or she fell. "Hooray! Goodbye!" the others shouted, and then I plunged into the air, waving. "Goodbye! Hooray!"

✝

When I got home, the house was dark. I yanked the door handle. It was locked, and I didn't have my key. I tried my shoulder against the door, twice, but it didn't give. I sat down on our front step, rubbing my shoulder. I didn't know where Clarissa would be staying. Her birch tree I'd planted sixteen years ago when we married looked scraggly. I must have stuck it in the ground wrong.

I got up and skulked around back. If worse came to worst, I'd sleep at my office. I never locked it. Pressing my face to the dining-room window, I tried to see the stairs to Clarissa's attic where she kept her knotted string of Peking glass beads, the miniature hands holding roses, one hand carved of ivory and one of bone. The glass steamed up. I was crying.

Don't make yourself miserable, I told myself. Sleep at your office. Leave her a message, in case she comes back. But I didn't have pen or paper. Mashing my lips against the glass, I murmured, "Clarissa, Clarissa." Maybe a short siege would help me see things in perspective. I'd write "Alton and Clarissa" in six-foot-high letters, emboss them in glass, giftwrap our names in a picture-window heart.

If I licked the glass a little, left a discreet tongue script, that would be something. She'd see my message was urgent, this symbol of what we'd created, signed with my tongue, sealed with my lips, home-delivered. An explorer reading the message of a fellow explorer, she'd see my struggle in each letter, each stroke of each letter. If she didn't, then to hell with her. I'd have done all a reasonable man can do.

I stuck my tongue out, testing the glass. I pulled it back in. Was it Puget Sound I tasted? In Alaska, hunters kill wolves by leaving knives in ice heaped with gobs of fat. A wolf finds the knife, licks it with numbed tongue until he rips his tongue to pieces and bleeds to death. Better be quick, I thought.

I dug in, then drew back. My letter *A* lay like two bent sticks, the crossbar between them squirmy and squeamish-looking. My tongue was unpracticed, a poor, blunt instrument. Oh, do it, I thought. Don't be such a damned perfectionist.

I licked the glass in bold, slashing strokes. Tomorrow I'd hate myself. I'd walk into class, thinking, "Go ahead, tell them. Alton Broome licks glass—licks it and likes it." But I wouldn't have to tell them that. A man's best and worst moments are his private possession, even when they're hard to tell apart. If he can't tell the sublime from the ridiculous, that's the price he pays for leaving his seal on the world.

I took a look at my work. It wasn't the best message a man ever put his tongue to. I liked the pure, wriggling look of the letter *C* in Clarissa. The heart I'd licked around our names resembled a baby whale, but I didn't care. I'd brought something new into the world.

I headed for my office, not forgetting to pick up the day's mail.

✝

Angel Hall has high, cool ceilings and bare pocked walls; flesh-colored ventilator pipes suck air in and out of the Chem labs, whooshing past a relief map of the Cascade Range. In my narrow, second-floor office, I sat, trying to think. Tomorrow, I'd go get my car. I'd left it on Commercial Street.

On my desk, between Clarissa's picture and one of my blue agates, lay a hardcover book: *Yes, I Don't Love You, Merlin,* by one Emily Weed. Funny title. My department chairman's ex-wife Thelma had left it for me. She'd mentioned the author, a visiting writer who teaches here at North Cascades, too. I glanced at the jacket notes. Short stories. On the cover, a woman wearing jeans and a blue-and-silver jacket walked away toward purple mountains.

I flipped to the last page, put my feet up on my desk, settled in. When I was ten, I read a book about a horse lamed by its cruel owner. Ever since, I've checked out endings first.

For a second, it was as if I were back in my parents' apartment in Riverdale, New York, near Spuyten Dyvil, where the Hudson and Harlem Rivers meet. Sitting on the windowsill, I used to read and wave to the man in the shack on the railroad bridge whom my mother called the man in the moon. His job was to open and close a drawbridge. Mine was to carry messages between my parents when they barricaded themselves in their rooms. On that day I read about the horse, my father's password had been "amalgamate"; my mother's had been "spirit guide."

Now I glanced up from the page. One of my remaining thundereggs glared at me from its shelf. Clarissa had carted my best rocks to the landfill just last week. Turning her picture face down, I flipped back to page one, a story called "Thanks." How could she say I don't take risks? Boldly, I began.

Eloise Hartwig stared at the wreck of her VW Bug, Brunhilda. Yellow flames went up, kind of pretty. She didn't believe in dying. But then she didn't believe in freeze-dried coffee, either. So what if someone was blowing up the clunkers of her friends in the Vegetarian League? So what if they had a CIA man in their midst? "Or a CIA woman," she muttered. She was pretty sure it wasn't her.

All right, a thriller, cars blowing up. I reached out for my thunderegg, pressed it to my lips. Eloise sounded different. She wouldn't cart a man's best rocks to the landfill. But why was she just "pretty sure" the double agent wasn't her?

The metal popped. A piece of soot brushed her lips. She spat. Damn the Dink. She didn't care if he was the head of the Vegetarian League. She had her other satellite lovers. So what if he did plan to kidnap the Secretary of Agriculture and release fifteen million beneficial insects if the League's demands to end the murder of animals weren't met? She had the clothes on her back, her blue satin oriental jacket, her jeans, her deerskin boots. She had the piece of dental floss she always kept taped to her wrist.

She started walking. With a loud boom, something picked her up in the air and threw her down flat.

She got up slowly. She was walking down a street. Holly Street. Brunhilda was... toast. Her house was... charred timbers, dust slowly rising. It was toast. Shit, shit, not a super day. She wiped her lips with one hand. It came away bleeding.

As she went past the Lighthouse Mission, she muttered, "Thanks," over and over.

I stood up. My scalp was prickly. In my mind, I saw her. *Toast,* what an expression. And she didn't believe in dying. What a brave spirit. And that "Shit, shit." Didn't that say it all? And her "Thanks." How mysterious. And she lived right here in Sehome!

My teeth chattering, I dropped the book. I was freezing. When I jammed my fists in my jacket pockets, something fell to the floor. I bent down. Scrawled on the back of a postcard of Mount Baker was the following:

Try Harder, Alton.
xxxxxxxx
Eloise

✛

I let out a cry. Be reasonable, I told myself. Women in stories didn't write postcards. But what about magnetic reversals? They happen, no one knows how.

Above her scrawl was a return address, the Miracle Laundromat. I turned the card over: Mount Baker, that snow dome, floating.

Today in number three, Clarissa had told me a dream she'd had six months earlier. We sat cross-legged on top of Mount Baker. A funnel-shaped cloud rolled out of a crevasse. The mountain exploded. She woke up, not upset, she said.

I groaned. Even her dreams warned her of coming reversals.

I made myself sit down, sit still. Opening the book, I turned to the next story, "Confessions of a Teenage Librarian." I winced; it wasn't funny. Eloise was in trouble. I went back to the table of contents: "Thanks," "Confessions," "Looking," "I Want You (With Apologies to B.D.)," "The Gecko," and "On the Road, Part One and Part Two."

I read "Confessions" straight through, getting facts and trying to see what geologists call the big picture. I went on, story after story, reading as I hadn't read since I was a child, not stopping until I came to the last paragraph of "On the Road, Part Two":

There was a roaring in her ears. She was walking down a beach. Black sand held her ankles and heels. Then the roaring was gone; it was inside her, a hollow churning, and the waves rolled in without sound. They were blue-black. They headed to a point. They rolled in with confidence, power, poise, with perfect measure. Something was over.

Throat burning, I shut the book, banged open my door, and ran down the dark hall to the department secretary's office—the Head Kick, our chairman Stevens called her. I swiped her campus directory, rifled pages. Warlock, Webber, Weed, half a dozen Weeds, no Emily, an E. Weed on 16 Diamond Street, no phone listed. Damn. I glanced at the wall clock. It was 3:13 a.m.

Back in my office, I scribbled the following:

November 8, 1985

Dear Miss Weed,

I've just finished your amazing book. I must thank you. Eloise is wonderful. In fact, I've fallen in love with her. Do you know where I can find her?

You see, I got this postcard. How can Eloise write me a postcard? I'm a man of facts. For sixteen years, ever since I got my Ph.D. and married Clarissa, facts have moved me along. My student evaluations are up there with Dr. Doll's, Dr. Sandman's, and Dr. Stevens'—Even Steven, we call him because he's so fair.

Lately, my wife and I have been meeting in our bank, trying to save our marriage. Now she's moved out, and I think this is it.

Miss Weed, I must confide more facts. My house is messy. The porch is sagging, the plaster is peeling, and I keep pots on top of the radiator to catch drops from the ceiling. The plants are dying.

The house is filled with the claptrap Clarissa and I
have collected. In sixteen years, you build up
memories. When I work in my basement on my
rocks, I look out at her birch tree. It makes the
friendliest noises in the wind.

    For Godsake, Miss Weed, I'm writing you from my
office. I'm locked out of my house.

Just for a second, I laid my head down on my desk. The
next thing I knew, I came awake with a jerk, head aching.
My watch said 5:37. I'd been having a dream.

Eloise and I were in New York. She carried her black
leather art portfolio, and I swept the street with a
pushbroom with stiff, black bristles. Near the Opera House
at Lincoln Center, I called out to her. I ran, sliding on white
stone. Waving a book in the air, she said, "It's my novel."

I picked up my pen and continued:

    Miss Weed, I had this dream. Talk about a character
coming to life. Eloise was waving her novel. You
haven't written a novel, have you?

    Please forgive my sedimentary tone. But the fact
is, my real life is going on somewhere else. I love
Eloise. I must find her!

Incautiously yours,
Alton Broome

✝

Grizzled, stomach growling, I put my missive in Emily's
tilted mailbox on Diamond Street at 6:10 a.m. The lights of
the boat harbor rippled under a gray dawn sky, and a
spruce tree with a double trunk swayed in the wind.

At eight o'clock, I taught my Intro class, keeping my
references to Eloise down to thirty-three during my lecture

on sedimentary rocks. In the afternoon, I wandered downtown. In Star Route Books on Holly Street, I checked out *Books in Print* and *Forthcoming Books in Print*, but found no listing for Emily Weed other than *Yes, I Don't Love You, Merlin*.

My car wasn't anywhere on Commercial Street. I got back on Holly, trudging through Old Town with its bars and junk shops, lowering my eyes when I went by the scrap metal yard and the Lighthouse Mission, built out of Chuckanut sandstone blocks. Near the Salvation Army Thrift Store, I saw her. Eloise.

The big E was big, with big hips, and small breasts pressed almost flat against a black T-shirt that said *WANT SOME?* The wind jaggedly parted her short, straight hair, flattening her brown bangs on one side. Her oriental jacket flapped happily, and she high-geared along, as if she could stride across continents or ride a horse over deserts and steppes and stretches of round, black stones—ride without looking back, leading a horde of ragtag children and desolate tribes, or running away from one. It was hard to tell which. Her wide-set eyes stared straight ahead, and her cheeks were puffy from the cold. The slogan on her T-shirt didn't do her justice. Eloise wasn't gross, she was direct. Even her breasts and hips looked direct.

As she turned to a long-haired man in jeans and a military jacket, she said, "Merlin, what do you mean it's 'lovely'? It's *gorgeous.*"

When she laughed, I knew it was her laugh.

Then she was gone. Merlin was gone. On the wet sidewalk where she'd stood lay my key ring with its disk of obsidian. I picked up my keys. A car backfired, and a black VW Bug with *Brunhilda* spraypainted in silver-blue roared off into the rain.

I started running, turned the corner onto Railroad Avenue. There, past the feed store, parked in front of Lerman's Pawnshop with its sign, *GUNS, GUITARS, TVs,*

VCRs, was my dented, white '63 Valiant. I got in and sat there, shaking.

✝

That night in my basement, I analyzed core samples. My deathless message had melted from the window. And no sign of Clarissa. Carefully, I blew into my blowpipe, sucking air in through my nose, as I peered at the edge of the flame for the color change that told me what I had. This was caveman geology, I used to tell Clarissa.

"Are you getting anything good?" she'd ask. Or in a matter-of-fact way, she'd say, "I'm all out of bloodstone. Beryl would be nice, too."

A frog-headed fellow, I waved gaily, then went back to huffing and puffing.

Just yesterday morning—was it yesterday?—she lay asleep on her side of our bed, wrapped in a sheet, mummyish. I loved her strong face, her big lips, big cheekbones. Her thin waist, her jutting hipbones, her thinness, then her fullness. On one bony shoulder, a mole was attached, loosely somehow. Her mouth was slack. Spittle pooled at one corner. Asleep, she accused me.

"I love you, Clarissa," I murmured.

She woke up, rubbing her fingers against her cheek. "Got to go to the Center. And to the vault."

The Center was where she worked as a therapist. The vault was where she kept her best jewelry.

"Why do you keep looking at your junk?" I asked.

"Not junk."

"Me, when I get my rocks labeled, I put them away."

She sat up. "Oh, you do not. You show them to Stevens."

"I used to," I admitted.

"Used to's all you two know."

✝

My flame had gone yellowish-green. The phone rang. I turned off the Bunsen burner, threw down my blowpipe, and took the basement steps three at a time. I picked up the phone. Out the window of the darkened living room, Clarissa's birch tree, lit by the porch light, trailed thin, sooty branches from its gray-white trunk, pristine and stark.

"Is this Alton Broome?" asked a woman, cutting off my vague hello.

"Yes."

"Emily Weed. I got your letter," she said in a clipped, accusing, slightly nasal voice that rose and held when she said "letter," as if she'd been expecting my message for some time.

"Sorry, I haven't been myself," I muttered, gazing up at a droplet that hung from my moldy ceiling.

"Your letter was super, Alton."

"Thanks," I said.

"Super" was Eloise's expression. This woman sounded older, but familiar somehow.

"No, thank *you.*" She clipped her words distinctly. "It's not every day a reader falls in love with Eloise. Tell me, what did you like about her?"

"Oh, everything, Miss Weed. I loved everything."

"Call me Emily," she said. "Alton, I don't know where you can find her. Is 'where' the right word? A relationship with a fictional woman has certain drawbacks, don't you see?"

"But I got this postcard—"

"I know, I know. Isn't that weird?"

She hummed something that resembled the theme music from *The Twilight Zone.* Then she went on in her rapid-fire way.

"Hey, what if the little snip pulled it off? I once said some shit about how my characters can decide what happens to them. Alton, you better watch out. She's very unpredictable. It's her character. I gave it to her. Hmm, I could kill her off. How'd that be?" She laughed.

"Kill her? Don't say that, Miss Weed."

"I will if you call me that one more time."

She sounded rueful, accusing, familiar. Why didn't she tell me how she knew me, like a reasonable woman? And I didn't care for her cursing; it was different from Eloise's somehow.

"Look, maybe I can help," I offered, frowning. "I'll meet her and soon I'll know things maybe you don't know."

"I don't need help, Alton. You do." Her laugh wasn't at all sweet. "Look, I'm willing to listen. Tell me about the bank, your rocks, your wife, whatever. If you sought professional help, frankly, they'd think you're bonkers."

"Maybe I am bonkers." I tightened the phone cord around my fist.

"I don't think so, Alton."

"You believe she's showing up here?"

"Wherever 'here' is," she said with a laugh.

I glanced up toward Clarissa's attic. The drop on the ceiling fell and hit my forehead.

"Miss Weed," I was blinking back grateful tears, "I'll search for her. Up and away. Hit the road."

"But where, Alton?" she asked in what I later termed her lost-cause tone of voice. "You can't just take off. Don't think —"

"I don't think anything." Clarissa had told me often enough what not to think.

"Can you meet me at the Sirocco, next Wednesday at noon? Please, Alton." She paused. "Shit, you're not making this easy for me."

The Sirocco was, and is, a restaurant. Wednesday was almost a week off.

"You can't make it sooner?" I blurted out.

"No, I can't. God, you assume an awful lot. You need a friend, Alton," she said kindly.

I swallowed hard. "How will I know you?"

"I'll know you."

"Wednesday. Thanks. Goodbye."

Her goodbye was sweet, clipped, oddly formal.

Cradling the phone, I took out Eloise's postcard and stared at her breath-taking scrawl.

TWO

I headed for the Miracle Laundromat on Lakeway near the hospital and the freeway. It's one of those open-twenty-four-hours jobs—where I went when Clarissa carted my rocks to the landfill. I had always liked the Miracle, even during my years before Clarissa—"B.C." I call them. In our early years, she did wash on the second and fourth Wednesday of each month, and I took the first, third, and fifth Wednesday when the month ran that way. During our seventh year, I protested.

"All those odd-numbered weeks I've been getting screwed," I said, and for a few months our marriage evened out.

At the Miracle, I liked to pick out a woman and pretend we were old lovers. There she'd be, folding her clean, fresh sheets, smoothing her jeans and T-shirts, hanging up blouses on hangers she'd brought from home. It didn't matter if they weren't wooden; plastic or wire was okay. I'd pretend we hadn't seen each other for years. I'd see myself saying, "My, you've fixed up the Miracle. You've painted it, haven't you? Those red and blue pipes painted onto the walls like racing stripes, and those big, white spigots painted on, too. I never did tell you I love you, did I? I was dumb back then. It *has* been years. Now when I go past the Miracle, that linty smell just drives me wild. Think of it, after all these years, you've kept things so nice and clean and new."

As I watched the sudsy shirts and sheets revolve in the washers, I tried to make plans. I couldn't lecture about my view of the ages and look for Eloise, too. I'd have to have it out with Even Steven—cry on his shoulder, tell him I needed a leave of absence.

It was past two a.m. when I left the Miracle and walked by Emily's place on Diamond Street. The fir trees notching the top of Sehome Hill were blacker than the sky. Behind white curtains in a lamplit upstairs window, a figure sat staring as if into a crystal ball. "Emily," I wanted to call out, "Can't I come up and see you?"

✟

On Friday morning, I caught a glimpse of Eloise standing by the claims department at Employment Security. She said to Merlin, "These state grants for unemployed artists are a super idea. I just love owning my own time. I can drink tea or paint or turn on the tube and catch one of the soaps."

But when I ran skidding across the tile floor, she wasn't there.

That night in the parking lot of a 7-Eleven, Eloise bragged to some high school kids about Merlin: "He can lift six-packs and walk out just like he's invisible." I crossed the street. A car screeched. She was gone.

In my Intro class on Wednesday morning, a dark-haired woman, older than the other students, frowned and stared oddly at me. After class I headed downtown. Smoke that smelled like coffee grounds billowed up from the pulp mill. The ornate white turret on top of the Mount Baker Theater resembled an antique wedding cake decoration, one from Precambrian time.

Near my bank on Commercial Street, catercorner from Star Route Books and the White Wolf New and Used Shop, I reached out to press the *WALK* button on a black lamppost. Across the street, sitting on the curb in the rain, staring at traffic was Eloise. The sign said *WALK*. She was gone.

On Indian Street downhill from the college, in a neighborhood Clarissa called the "student slums," I saw a woman on a porch, or I saw her bottom half. A long trailing ivy hid her face and shoulders. A black velvet coat floated to her knees. The woman inched around the ivy like a kid trying to hide behind a tree.

"Eloise?"

As I ran up the steps, the woman popped her head out, smiling. She had round black eyes, full cheeks, and big, spilling breasts. I think you'd have to say she had a bosom—or is it bosoms? How can "bosom" be both singular and plural? Women are so mysterious. "Boobs" is what Eloise says. She's direct.

"Dammit, you're not Eloise." I flailed an arm.

"Sorry," she said evenly. "Who's Eloise?"

"Oh, just someone I read about in a story—in six short stories, as a matter of fact. Let's not talk about it. Let's drop the subject."

"This is a new one." She laughed. "This is a line, isn't it?"

I turned my coat collar up. I thought it would look tough.

"Well, how are you going to recognize your honey, if you don't mind my asking? You must have a great imagination."

"Oh, no. Just average. For one thing, Eloise wears a blue satin oriental jacket, and she's fond of smoked oysters, and she's very careful about brushing."

"Smells like smoked oysters and toothpaste?"

"Tooth *powder*. She flosses thirty minutes a day—keeps a piece of dental floss taped to her wrist like a hospital I.D. bracelet. What are you doing, by the way?"

"I'm repotting this monster. Swedish ivy, the last tenants left it. You wouldn't happen to know someone looking for an apartment, by the way?"

"No, I don't. And I've got to get busy, or I'll never find Eloise," I said. "So goodbye."

Miss Bosom smoothed down the sides of her velvet coat. "Say hi to Eloise for me if you catch up with her."

"You know her then?"

"No, I just believe you're doing what you say you are. I don't know why, but I do. Let me know. I like hearing success stories."

"Good luck with the monster." I turned my coat collar down.

☦

At noon in the Sirocco on Lakeway, not far from the Miracle, a woman wearing a long, purple paisley skirt and a magenta turtleneck sat down at my table.

"Emily?"

"Hi, Alton." She had a straightforward, door-opening face, not pretty, too many corners and angles. She had dark, curly hair. Her green-brown eyes, crinkled at the corners, were warm. Maybe she was thirty, thirty-five.

Her half-smile widened as she pointed to my glass of water. "Do you mind? I'm thirsty."

She downed the water and set the glass down with a clatter. Over a fake potted palm tree, a black ceiling fan spun listlessly. Glancing up, she said with a laugh, "Jeez, it looks like something from *Casablanca*, doesn't it?"

A turbanned waiter brought menus. I ordered what she did, and he whisked himself away like a desert wind. Emily patted back a few strands of hair from her damp, bony forehead. She frowned, her dark eyes intent, and I remembered.

"Emily, you're Miss Weed, aren't you? In my 201 class? I've poured out my secrets. And to who? To whom? To someone who *knows* me, of all things."

I studied her old-looking eyes. "You must think I'm really loony," I blurted out. "Or are you here looking for material?"

"No, Alton." Sighing, she waved one hand as if to qualify what she said, then went on in her precise, clipped voice. "I think you know what I want to tell you. Give up on her."

"But Emily—"

"She'd only disappoint you. She's a figment of your— or I should say *my* imagination." She raised one hand, let it fall. "I hate to tell you, but Eloise, the great artist? She paints by numbers. She started in a paint-by-number correspondence school. Dotted lines, the whole bit. It'd hurt her to find out her school isn't the cubist movement."

"But she's adorable, offbeat."

"You don't think you're being a bit naive?"

My mouth dropped open.

"But you are," she went on, "and it hurts me. People don't jump off the deep end like this. You don't say the devil made you do it or your shrink told you it's okay. You just say you're looking for a woman who doesn't exist. Terrific. I wish you luck on your escapade."

"Escapade?"

"Well, maybe a fling will do you good. You know, she runs around her apartment naked, yelling, 'Shit, shit, my roof is leaking, and my Canadian landlord won't fix it. Damn Canadians. They come down to Sehome and clog up traffic and buy all the land, and all they ever say is, "Do you know how to get to K-Mart?"' I didn't put that in the stories, Alton. Do you know she has five lovers right now, not counting Merlin?"

"I know she's fiery, vivacious, spirited. Can't you tell me where she is?"

"Alton, she's a character in some stories. Can't you get that through your head?"

"But don't you think we'd *make* a good story? Eloise and me. We'd meet, talk in this funny or uplifting way. I don't want to be in a story that isn't uplifting, or at least funny."

Emily let out her breath. "You want me to put you in a story so you can rub noses with her, tickle and stroke her and tell her the most adorable shit that you—or I—can think of?"

Yes, oh yes.

"You want me to be your Travel Lodge, your Bide-a-wee Motel? Well, I won't do it. For six months I haven't written a damned thing." She paused. "You're not going to see her!"

"But I have seen her, Emily," I said mildly, my face hot.

"You have?" She sounded aghast yet oddly hopeful.

"Seen her and heard her, right here in town. I know you've imagined her. Think of it, she's words on a page, and then those words jump off the page. Aren't you writers always hoping your characters come to life?"

Glassy-eyed, Emily took a sip of water.

"Her laugh isn't *exactly* how you described it. It's kind of rippling, yes. Am I misquoting you?"

She put down her glass and picked up her napkin, twisting it as if it were a tourniquet.

"Oh, she's got a wonderful laugh. It started with a tee-hee, but then she broke up. A real uproar, like she was up on stilts and someone tipped her forward and she had to keep on going."

Emily was methodically shredding the napkin.

"Her laugh, it was, I don't know, an embroidered laugh, all these fancy stitches spreading confidently. Ricochets and things. I mean, it was a pleasant laugh."

I have a teacher's habit of taking peeks at people as I talk. "Pulling the string," Stevens calls it.

When I looked up, Emily was crying, wiping her eyes precisely, first one hand, then the other. She threw down her napkin, what was left of it.

"I don't think I can help you, Alton," she said in a clipped, pained voice, and she got up.

I stood; my chair tottered but didn't fall. Our waiter, old desert wind, dropped a plate. People stared.

Reaching across the table, I grasped her elbow. "Please, Emily, you offered me your friendship."

With an angry sigh, she sat back down. I did, too.

"Couldn't you try and write a story about us?" I asked.

"Couldn't *you* try, Alton? Try not believing in her." She gave me a crooked smile.

So she'd been humoring me. I thought we were in this together—her writing, me reading. Granted, I was forty and close to divorced, with not much to show but what was left of my rocks. I knew it was cuckoo to look for Eloise.

"Emily, crazy things are happening all the time. Wars, volcanos. I even went to a shrink the other day."

It was a fact.

"What happened? You didn't like him?"

"I didn't like *her*. She was a woman. Is still a woman. I couldn't break it to her about Eloise, and she got bored. She said, 'We'll stop here' the way I do after I've run through my definition of igneous rocks. It was awful."

"Alton, I'd write a story if I could, but I can't."

Then she frowned and got less pretty and that scared me.

For a second, I was back in my class, writing "geosyncline" on the blackboard, chalk on my cuffs, my students with their eyes vacant, their windowshades pulled down, all except one woman, this woman. *She's a writer*, I thought. *She gets readers to pay attention. Me, the kind of life I lead, it's as if I didn't exist.*

"I know you're in pain, Alton." She bowed her head slightly.

"So there was one student who learned that fact. We both know who she was—"

"And is," she said softly.

"I couldn't ever thank that student enough. But Emily, don't you see, this is my one chance to get away from the wolves, the vault. Just wipe it all out."

It hit me, what awesome responsibilities a man in a story has.

"But there is a real world out there, Alton."

"Can you understand why...?"

"I know about making new starts," she said with a pinched, sad smile.

I wanted to tell her things would work out. She'd write again. Me, I'd come back from looking for the big E like a man coming off a binge. Refreshed, you know. But something told me it wasn't going to be that easy, not for her or for me, either. My odyssey—or I should say my idiocy—was waiting for me.

"Will you write, Emily? Letters, I mean." I didn't know where my search would take me.

"I'll write you," she said.

"If you don't write stories for a while, don't worry. I have faith in you."

"Thanks," she said. Formal. Polite. Even the way she straightened her shoulders seemed polite. She smiled, a beautiful smile, even though it was bigger on one side than the other.

"You're welcome," I said.

We both looked down at our empty water glasses. It was time for me to hit the fictional road.

THREE

I marched up the hill to ask Stevens for a leave of absence. Even Steven was a young fifty-four. His first name was Stanley, but everyone called him Stevie or Dr. Stevens. I wasn't thrilled with either one, so I depended on eye contact, respectfully-raised eyebrows, and lots of nodding.

He was a happy-looking man—serene, dry, Olympian. Everything struck him funny in a remote way. He had sleepy, slow-blinking eyes and a sandy mustache that was a new addition. Stevens was always remodeling his face, adding beard or mustache, then chopping off the new growth and reseeding. When one of his boughs grew back, he liked to fondle it.

Stevens was my mentor. My advisor in grad school in New York, he was the one I went to when things went wrong—when my students stole my desk, when I lost my semester's class notes, and lately when Clarissa and I had a scene. Even Steven had raised me from a pup, he said.

The first time I talked to him in New York, he'd said, "Continental drift is rearing its ugly head. Trench warfare, even steven, no holds barred."

I nicknamed him on the spot. Our department had been in an uproar. The fit of South America and Africa like puzzle parts, the match of their fossil and rock records—geologists had known about that for a long time. But now the paleomagicians said the magnetic lines laid down in the rocks two hundred million years ago point to two different North Poles, but if you snug Africa and South America up close, the lines point to one north. Thus Pangaea, the one super-continent, big as life.

When Stevens left to take the position of chairman here at North Cascades, he invited me to apply as an instructor. I asked if you could see water from the college.

"Water and mountains, too," he said. "Mild winters. Lots of mist. Fine if your bent is absent-mindedness, as mine is."

☦

Stevens' office, a shrine I tried not to visit too often, got remodeled about as often as his face did. Today the place was heaped with beams, two-by-fours, and tin cans full of nails. He'd knocked out a wall to make a suite so he could move in his practice piano that made a knocking sound like a radiator. On top of the practice piano sat his massive paperweight of banded bull's-eye malachite.

Stevens published a book and half a dozen articles a year. Before they divorced, Thelma used to hand-letter notes of the events that read like birth announcements. I always got depressed on days when her notes came in the mail.

"Could I speak to you?" I whispered loudly. "It's confidential."

Through a haze of sawdust, Stevens gave me a boyishly aloof grin. "Family matters is it, Alton, in point of fact?"

That was his pet expression, "in point of fact." In grad school once, I counted how many times he used it in a lecture. The score was twenty-seven in just thirty minutes. He'd dismissed class early that day.

Stevens was also a hand rubber. He brushed his fingers together, nestling the knuckles for just the right fit. Then he held up his hands and examined his fingernails critically, rubbing his thumb over each nail, testing for rough edges.

"Did you know I wanted to be a concert pianist, Alton?" he asked.

No, I didn't know that.

"My mother said I could do that or be a brain surgeon." He grinned a you're-not-the-only-one-who's-got-troubles grin.

"Must have been rough."

He shook his head. "It was. Mama couldn't see my fingers are on the, shall we say, short side? 'You have long beautiful fingers, Stanley,' she always said. After my first concert appearance in college, I told her who I am—Stevens, in point of fact, Stevie for short. 'Mama,' I said, 'this solid earth is hopping, and I want to find out how rocks are bedded and faulted and folded and layered. Mama, think of metamorphic rock. It's buried in the juices of the earth—gassed and cooked and pressed until those billion-year-old faces wear an expression of humility and sympathy—yes, sympathy for the earth that rocked them, milked them with magma, transformed them into new rocks.'"

He stroked his mustache, a gleam in his gray eyes. "By the way, Alton, rocks are quite sexy—or maybe you've heard me on this subject? No? What a superb orifice the Grand Canyon is. Wouldn't you love to fill it with good, juicy knowledge? All those layers—the Temple Butte, Redwall Limestone. I want to plug all the holes I can find, plug them, hug them, lug them home. I told Mama my fingers are stubby, Alton, yes, stubby, and amazingly that metamorphosed our relationship. She said she hoped I'd find a cavity worthy of me. She still calls me Stanley, though."

What in the world are we talking about? I thought. I came here to talk about *me*. Stevens' fingers rested quietly in the faults they were destined for. How even his nails were. My nails looked as if they'd been stripmined. If I had nails like his, I'd chow down on one hand and save the other one for show—keep one hand in my pocket, wear a black glove, say I had an infectious skin condition.

"Alton, we do go on, in point of fact," he said, gazing at me kindly.

"Well, I'm sorry to hear that." I didn't know what I meant. It slipped out. "Stevie," I said suddenly. "Can I call you that? I've realized something. About Clarissa, teaching, the whole thing. I need to pack it in, take a leave of absence for a year."

He pressed his knuckles down against his desk. "Pack it in? Are you joining the Me Generation?" He sounded concerned in a dry sort of way, yet relieved. His eyes had narrowed and his lips had pursed when I mentioned Clarissa.

"You see, I don't exist. Not really," I explained, waving away his look of protest. "My student who's flunking wrote me a note begging me to pass him. He addressed the note, 'To Whom It May Concern.'"

He smiled. "Standards aren't what they used to be, Alton. Don't feel bad. He probably had three or four other letters like that to write."

"But Stevie, I met a woman."

"Alton, I'm delighted. First, that you call me Stevie—after all these years. And now to hear you're making new friends in this trying time of your life—in point of fact, I think it's neat. Are you and she on intimate terms? Do you see each other often?"

"Not very often." I paused. "We're in the initial, critical stages. It's puppy love—I've been following her around."

Stevens rolled his eyes.

"Miss B, I'll call her—she's my imaginary friend. She doesn't exist either. Stevie, my real life is going on somewhere else. I have to find it. And Clarissa, you see—she's gone, again."

Stevens' knuckles were white.

"Oh, Stevie," I broke down, crying. "She's gone so many

times. I never thought she'd ever, you know, just *go*."

Sixteen years ago, I'd met Clarissa when she handed me a survey on sex attitudes. The next week, she stumbled into the emergency room at St. Luke's Hospital, holding an empty bottle of pills, working one arm like a swimmer, parting the air. Eyes big and starey. I'd chipped a bone in my ankle. I sat waiting for my plaster cast to dry.

"You took six? Or sixty?" the attendant asked her.

The next day, I'd gone to see her. As I hobbled up in my walking cast, I said brightly, "Excuse me, you should finish that sex attitude survey you started."

Seven years later, she did. It was her thesis, *Symbiosis and Sex: A Cross-Cultural Survey.* I'd never minded her asking all the time if I felt cared for. It was reassuring.

‡

"I think I'm going nuts, sir," I said to Stevens. "What do you think?"

"Alton, you sound depressed. In point of fact, I'd say you sound desperate."

"Oh, I am, I am," I said brightly. It felt so good to be understood. Shaking, I narrowed my fingers into a steeple and wiggled them. "Here's all the nutty people," I said.

"Alton, what are you feeling? Right now, at this moment, in point of fact?"

"I feel awful."

"Good, good. I'm glad you can express that. A man in your straits should be feeling awful."

He gave me a dry, happy-to-be-of-service grin.

"But it *isn't* good," I said. "Just last week she came back again. Beamed when I walked in the door—hugged me and called me her old Rock of Ages."

Stevens' grin looked dessicated now, not happy.

"She'd tossed one of her seven-salad wonders—spinach leaves and wheat germ and peanut oil and red lettuce and mandarin oranges and kiwies and olives and chives and bulgar wheat and marinated sunflower seeds."

"Went all out?"

"She even pinned a flower in her hair, so I hardly noticed her ears sticking out like I usually do. Cooing in that confidential way she has—"

I paused. He nodded.

"Well, she told me her salad was invented by a friend of hers, an educational psychologist named Norwood Whacker? She rolled her tongue over a half-chewed tomato. What could I say? I kept looking at her, a long look."

"You were communicating?"

"Oh, yes."

Stevens pursed his lips and expelled a dusty, Mesozoic sigh. His knuckles should have been metamorphosed to travertine by now.

He shook his head, sighing. "It's been a long time, Alton. You and Clarissa—a long time." A tear rolled down the runnel of his right cheek. "I don't think I can help you, Alton."

Emily had said that, too. Now Stevens was wiping off the solitary tear with a bony knuckle. He eyeballed the wet knuckle, as if awed by it.

"You and Clarissa have been at North Cascades for how many years now?"

"Sixteen years."

"And what does Clarissa teach? I forget." His low voice was lulling, but his eyelids jumped like grasshoppers.

"She doesn't teach—she counsels—in point of fact." I was trying to wake him with his pet expression.

He gazed at his bull's-eye malachite. "Academic or psychological?"

"Psychological!" I shouted.

Was he trying to gaslight me? He knew Clarissa. They'd seen each other plenty when she was setting up her real estate practice. They even wrote an article together: "Geology and Real Estate: Strange Bedfellows."

"*Stanley*," I said pointedly, "is there something you're not telling me?"

Stevens expelled a sigh that seeped down to me from four billion years ago.

"I'm going to be brutally honest with you, Alton. In point of fact, Clarissa and I are seeing each other."

I pictured them—Clarissa holding his bony knuckles or Stevens fiddling her, fondling her, fingering her.

"I know you two see each other," I said brightly. "What's the big deal?"

Stevens gazed at his practice piano.

"Do you mean, are you two screwing around?"

"Well, yes, Alton." He grinned the driest little grin, as if it were a good joke, just between the two of us.

I'll kill him, I thought. *Rub him in sawdust, knock out his keys. Soundproof him. Point-of-fact him. Click-clack. I'll nail the bastard.*

"How long?"

"The whole sad sixteen years, Alton."

Nothing was coming out of me, just dry heaves. I was breathing like crazy, but I couldn't breathe. Just sawdust came in. Even Steven was staring at his bull's-eye malachite, as if at an expensive, primitive idol. His practice piano gleamed. Fingers pressed together, he resembled a big, blond, aging praying mantis. I was heaving away, and then I blacked out. When I came to, I was on the floor and Stevens was on the phone.

"Yes, you'd better.... Refer him to someone, Clarissa.... Yes, that's appropriate."

My forehead ached. When I dabbed at it with my sleeve, the wool and sawdust stung. I was bleeding. I should have stayed at the Miracle, watching the suds, dreaming of Eloise, where everything was nice and clean and real.

✠

But I didn't go to the Miracle. I headed for Clarissa's office in the Counseling Center. The receptionist gave me an odd look when I staggered in.

"Do you want to make an appointment?" she asked.

"No, I want to see my wife. Clarissa."

"Do you have an appointment?"

"No, I want a word with her." I pressed my forearm to my head.

The receptionist held down a button and punched three numbers. "I'm sorry, she's with a client."

"Can you make sure she gets this message? I'm Alton Broome, her husband. I'd like to meet her at the vault at exactly 3:30 p.m. in point of fact. Have you got that—*in point of fact*. Make sure and write that down. And that's 'vault' with a lower-case 'v'. Have you got that?"

I said that about the 'v' to avoid confusion with a local bar Clarissa wouldn't be caught dead in. I don't know why I used Stevens' pet expression. The receptionist seemed to take a long time writing, maybe adding a few choice words of her own.

"Never seen blood before?" I growled in my best James Cagney voice, pulling my coat collar up.

A young woman with short brown hair and a wide face was sitting in the waiting room, staring up over a *People* magazine. She wore jeans, deer-skin boots, and yes, a blue satin oriental jacket. She looked worried, drawn, and tired.

"Eloise!" I cried. "It *is* you."

She started to cry quietly. I sat down next to her, covering my forehead with one hand. I didn't want her thinking I was some creep who couldn't stay out of fights.

"Eloise, what's the matter?"

The receptionist shot me a scared look.

"Alton, she can't see me," said Eloise in a faint voice. "I've been trying so hard to be real, turning up in all the likely places—junk shops, thrift shops, the sewage treatment plant at Marine Park. I fill out forms at Employment Security. It's not fair."

As the receptionist made a headlong exit, I put my arm around Eloise's shoulder.

"No, I can't keep this up for long. Don't look at me."

I glanced down at the *People* magazine cover, on which was some cleavage and a headline, "This Time Will It Last?"

"Alton, you better get out of here. That receptionist means business."

"Oh, Eloise, I want to breathe you in. You're my fresh air. You can't believe the day I've had."

"I can guess," she said, looking me over.

I breathed in the scent of smoked oysters and tooth powder.

"Eloise, I want to tear off a piece of your silk jacket and wear it like a pennant."

"That's sweet, Alton. But what you could use is a bandage. What did you do to yourself? Don't tell me. Just let me look at you a second. Oh, Alton, this is all so crazy."

"I talked to Stevens," I said. "I asked him for a leave of absence. I'm putting a *GONE FISHING* sign on my office door."

"That's a super idea, Alton," she said in her scratchy voice. "I'm going to take lots of your time now. So far I've been popping up on streets and in stores and offices. Pretty soon I'll be up to homes and apartments. Oh, please take care of yourself, Alton. I've got to split now. I feel it coming. Please have the decency to turn away. I'm not the sort of person who fades into the woodwork."

And she was gone. I picked up the *People* magazine and pressed it to my forehead. I'd finally bumped into the big E. The world of the imagination was turning out to be a small town after all.

I ran to my office, put up my *GONE FISHING* sign, and headed for the vault with a small 'v.'

Four

At Cascadia Commercial, the safe deposit boxes were downstairs at the end of a white hallway. Rows of numbered boxes slept behind bars as if they'd been ruled dangerous. The large, bald, uniformed guard sat at a glittering dark table in front of the steel-barred door. Mr. Vault glanced up, rubbing his forehead and licking his thick lips a little.

"Come to fondle the valuables?" he boomed in an offhand yet amused way, his tongue showing like a bulldog's. Sitting by his gate to this steely underworld, he peered at me over an open leather notebook, as if he knew why I came here.

"Well, *did* you?" he asked.

"I'm here to meet my wife." I felt his eyes on me as I signed his book.

He checked my signature, then took out another book from his desk drawer, Moody's *Guide to Common and Preferred Stocks.* Opening it, he said, "Wife, yes. But facts first. Can I interest you in Tiger International? Or Stokely Van Camp, that's closer to home." Reading aloud, he quoted, "'Frozen food products are directed to higher profit margins.' Excellent prospects. You know about prospects, do you?"

Will you just let me in?" I dabbed at my cut forehead.

"Just a few words from the faithful Moody first. How about Growth Diamonds? Excellent prospects."

"Let me in!" I was practically shouting.

Mr. Vault rubbed his bumpy forehead. When he got up and clanked his steel door open, I followed, holding my deposit box key and tiptoeing in. Rows of boxes lined three walls of the vault, silver numerals glittering on black tabs at the corner of each box. The far wall held three numbered doors with red and green lights above them. A green light meant that cubicle was unoccupied and you could go in and dust off your valuables.

Mr. Vault inserted my key and his duplicate into their slots, taking out Clarissa's and my long, thin wafer of a box from its slot.

"Would you please tell Mrs. Broome I'm in number one?"

"Mr. B in number one for Mrs. B," he barked, handing me the box. "Mum's the word. Just remember, facts and prospects."

I opened number one and sat down at a white formica counter in front of a large wall mirror. A recessed ceiling light cast an orange glow like a sulphur lamp or something from a motel bathroom. Good old number one. Only five by seven feet, it brought back memories, this familiar inner sanctum.

I slid the oblong lid from Clarissa's and my deposit box and looked inside. Her ring was there, no surprise. We'd taken our rings out just last week and put them back on again after a tearful reunion here in number one. Then, later in the week, we'd taken off our rings again in number three. I'd put mine back on after Clarissa left.

Now I tugged the gold band from my ring finger. A bit of dried blood stained the gold, and I licked it as I waited. A salty taste—maybe it was the blood, or maybe perspiration. I licked until the salt went away and I was tasting our white gold. I thought of when I'd gone back to our house and licked our names onto the glass. I'd tasted the same saltiness then.

I set the gold ring down beside the empty deposit box in front of the mirror. My ring looked small but significant, like one of those immaculate, tiny icons you move around a Monopoly board—the Iron or the Car. This was the Ring. I nudged it a little, squinting at myself in the mirror.

Clarissa always said I had a mask face, a flat face, a good old Rock of Ages face. The man I saw looked dazed and fortyish. His forehead had taken a bad cut. His flat nose looked as if the continental plates of his skull had only been able to budge that nose an inch or so up from the stolid mass of his flesh.

I closed my hand on my ring until it hurt. I won't think about her, I told myself. I won't. I scrunched my eyes tight, letting out a howl.

"Eloise, why aren't you here to help me?" I shouted. "You just pop up whenever you feel like it. It's not fair."

If she were here with me in number one, Eloise would probably say, "Alton, what're you doing in this dumb closet?" I'd look at her for a second, and she'd say, "This is something that has to be?"

I nodded at the mask face in the mirror and put my wedding ring back on. Though Clarissa and I had met here for reunions five times before, I had no hope of a sixth time. I clamped my teeth tight and said, "I want the truth."

I wanted it, and it had damn well better set me free, I thought. Clarissa and I would have an amicable chat in good old number one. No more heroics. No more excising our rings, tossing them in each other's faces, or tearfully putting them back on. No more throwing our rings down furiously and then hugging and making up in ten seconds flat. No more tantrums, no feature-length reunions. No more saying, "How lonely the poor things look," as we stared at our rings on the floor. No more saying, "We both sure have beautiful eyes," or "We've spoiled each other good. We won't find lovemaking like we've found."

Instead we'd have a friendly chat. Clarissa would stare at me with her gray eyes and say, "So this is it." She'd probably coo a bit breathily the way she does. "Maybe in some other world—maybe in twenty or thirty years when we're both sadder, but much, much wiser, we'll meet again and say to each other, 'Isn't wisdom better than all that passion and lust?'"

"Wisdom and passion *and* lust," I growled at the mask face in the mirror, thinking twenty or thirty years isn't a long time on any time-scale a geologist is used to, yet it is a long time.

"Oh, Clarissa," I said to the empty deposit box, "how could you? And with Stevens who's in love with his own stubby little fingers. Why'd you let him slip it to you all of our sixteen years?"

✜

One time in number three, I asked her why. If I knew why, I could put that in the deposit box at least.

"I'm no good for you, Alton," she said, making her eyes big.

"But you are. Why? Why?"

She stared at me, her lips trembling as her gaze held steady, her big gray eyes glittering softly like the numerals on our deposit box, infinitely precious and valuable. Something was happening to her. Her eyes looked ready for something awful to pop out of them. They were her hospital eyes, her eyes the way I'd seen them when she was wheeled past me sixteen years ago. Overdose eyes, spirit eyes, eyes full of the last things. I wanted to wrap a blanket around us both, to rub her feet, to warm her freezing fingers in my hands.

"I feel cold, Alton," she said, eerily anticipating me.

I reached out and held her.

"Empty and cold," she said as I rocked her.

☦

That first time I'd spoken to her in the hospital, she'd said, "Are you my doctor? Are you my father?"

"No, I'm Alton Broome. You interviewed me. Your sex attitude questionnaire? You said I was a find."

"I feel dead," she murmured, staring off down the shiny, white corridor past a woman in a tan bathrobe.

"You don't look dead," I said brightly.

She nodded, focused her eyes, then let them get big. We started down the corridor toward the solarium.

"It's the drugs they give me," she said sonorously yet as if by rote. "Thorazine makes me feel dead. But I'm getting better and better every day."

"I'm sure you are," I said.

The next day I brought her chocolates and magazines. When she got day passes, we went for drives, bought lots of food, and rode to Larrabee Park where we climbed to the lookout point to see all the islands roll out into Puget Sound, layer on layer, all those blue hills folding into each other.

"The San Juan Islands are an archipelago," I said cheerfully.

"I know."

When we drove back to town, we bought fat green peppers at the farmers' market, and we sliced them into salads at Clarissa's apartment. We ate strawberries with whipped cream for dessert. We painted Clarissa's apartment yellow. After she was released from the hospital, I visited her in the morning and cooked her omelettes with mushrooms, onions, bacon, and three kinds of cheese. We walked over the railway trestle to the beach on the south side of town. Spindly black pilings left over from an abandoned sawmill stood tilting, worn away by water at the base. A section of a cedar log ten feet in diameter lay like a giant's thighbone wrenched from its socket. Snaky, bulbous kelp looked deranged, a shiny leapfrog green. It was cold on the beach, so we sat in the car until the windows steamed and Clarissa started crying and I held her.

"It's been so hard for me to come this far," she said.

The first time Clarissa and I made love, we climbed up to her yellow-gold room by a back stairway, picking our way past a bicycle, a half-dead rubber plant, and piles of clothes, books, and stuffed pillows strewn on the floor of her room.

She was nineteen; I was twenty-four. Although this was my first time, I'd done a lot of reading on the subject, so I knew it often took men a shorter time to reach orgasm than it takes women. Putting me into her quickly, Clarissa moaned, tugging on my shoulders until I went all the way in. Jerking and working her pelvis like a lever, she strained, gasped, and then more suddenly than I expected, she collapsed all around me like loose earth crumbling, moaning once. Then she went slack.

After a minute, she asked, "Was it good for you?"

"Um," I said definitely.

"You didn't come, did you?"

"No," I said, a bit less definitely.

She was crying. "Oh, Alton, I'm sorry. I wanted your first time to be good for you."

"It was. It was very nice," I said brightly, kissing her cheek and patting her shoulder.

"Well, next time you move, too, okay?" she said. "But not just for a little while yet, please."

✠

After she got out of the hospital, Clarissa slowly came back to life. She finished college, started graduate school, and went through seven years of therapy. We both began a steady climb. I had never thought a reasonable man could be so happy. We almost never had fights. I had my classes and my rock collection. Clarissa had her clients at the Counseling Center, and she worked in earnest on her jewelry collection. Our time together was brief, but it was quality time, we both agreed.

When Clarissa started collecting antique jewelry, she got a jewelry box she plumped her stuff in. That, a dealer told her, was a deplorable practice, and she soon had cases made of leather and silk that she kept in her attic study.

She said, "When I saw what I'd done to my poor old pieces—cracked agates, dented lockets—I felt like I'd been violated. I've been taking lousy care of them."

Soon she had display cases made—glass boxes inside more glass like a mathematician's construct of an imaginary universe.

I liked to go up to her attic sometimes when she was working at the Counseling Center. How Clarissa had changed from a patient to a therapist amazed me. I didn't think I could change in seven years or seven hundred years. I'd always be the solid man of facts I'd been.

The skylight Stevens had helped us put in pulled in light and spilled it purely on the white attic walls. The bay shone. The purple islands shouldered themselves cleanly out of the soft, gray water. How at peace I felt when I stole into Clarissa's world, gazing at her glass cases filled with beads, her butterscotch amber necklace, the black amber with the pendant carved rose, the strand of black Peking glass beads with knotted cords and a tasseled fringe.

There were cases of so-called rare objects: pieces of bog oak with dragonflies carved on them, a ruby glass brooch, an aquamarine griffin, a lock-and-key bracelet, a jade goddess holding a sea horse, and the two miniature hands holding roses, one hand carved of ivory and one of bone.

And later there were her most precious possessions: a five-turn, ruby and diamond serpent ring, its two gold heads wrapped around each other; a Brazilian emerald brooch; her Cocochat fighting fish, its gold enamel extending to the fins; and her Afghan necklace of lapis lazuli, its heart-shaped pendant cut cleanly in two.

I used to feel I had a kind of peerless pirate bride for a wife, pillaging the antique stores and jewelry dealers, bringing home tribute and spoils. I was sure there had to be a story for each piece—one about the emperor who had the Peking glass beads made and one about the hands carved from ivory and bone.

When I asked Clarissa if any of her patients at the Counseling Center ever gave her a ruby brooch or a jet mourning ring, she said, incredulously, "Alton, my clients are students." She said the word "students" as if I should know they couldn't afford to give her such gifts.

‡

Even after Clarissa decided she needed a safe deposit box to store her most valuable pieces, she still kept stashes at home: brooches in plastic bags tucked away in a corner of the freezer, rings in baggies hidden at the bottom of the clothes hamper. Many a time we went on treasure hunts to find irreplaceable pieces that had disappeared from inside the washer or dryer or the cuckoo clock that no longer kept time or from inside my rolled-up socks or the boles of pipes.

Before long Clarissa became what she called a serious collector. She didn't lose things anymore, or hardly ever, and she didn't have time to answer questions put to my pirate bride.

"A lover of fine things must learn to tell fact from fiction," she said once as she put a brooch in a case in her attic. "I'm not talking about primary jewelry—not diamonds and pearls. I'm not there yet. I mean day jewelry, the kind of stuff you can pick up for five or ten dollars." Standing under the skylight, she glanced at her case of rare objects. "Of course, they can go up to one thousand, or even more, if they have beauty and workmanship. The investment isn't the only reason I do it, though. You see, a collector must be as attentive as a lover. You've got to take your strings of pearl out to let them breathe. You've got to check your pieces for cracking and warping. A collector has got to be even more careful than a lover, Alton. A lover, well, he tries to please, but does he do it? I'm just saying 'he' for argument's sake. I could say 'she.' She tries to help, to set him straight. I'm not talking about us, Alton. It's just that jewelry repays avid attention. Pearls get pearlier when you wear them. Opals warm against your throat. Jade changes color on your wrist."

How logically, how patiently she explains things, I thought. The way her mind worked made me feel safe. I felt touched, even though I *didn't* understand as I gazed into her wraith-gray eyes.

✝

Two months ago when we put our rings back on in number one, I knelt and kissed Clarissa's belly.

"No, I can't breathe." She pulled back, and her eyes fixed me, staring from a place where galaxies had once exploded but where now was just cold space.

"Are you sure you're feeling okay?" I asked cautiously.

"Are you?" she shot back. "You've always treated me like I'm sick. Well, I'm not sick."

Her eyes were letting off salvos; then they softened.

"Alton, we're in hell," she said calmly.

I looked around for a second to make sure of where we were. There were the two of us in the mirror under the orange ceiling lamp. There was our empty deposit box, our rings.

"I love you, Clarissa. I don't understand a word you're saying."

"That's what I mean."

Numbly I said, "I'm a man of facts. I can't ever understand all you do. But we've got something. It's like a chemical—" I glanced down at the cold white tile floor. I didn't know how to say it, but I was thinking of the chemical bond that forms when magma forces heat into rocks, scouring gneiss and granite with gases and molten rock moving under great pressure until new, important products—minerals and gemstones—are formed.

When I looked up, Clarissa was staring at me as if I were from some other planet, the way my students did.

"A chemical? Are you telling me you love me, Alton?"

"Yes!"

"But do you care for me, truly care for *me*?"

I reached for her and tried to nuzzle my head up her belly to her breast.

"Look at me, Alton. Why can't you bear to look at me?"

"I can bear it," I said.

"Oh, you're so insulting. You can *bear* it."

"I'm sorry, Clarissa. I didn't mean it. I don't know what you want me to say. You're my good angel. Tell me. You've studied enough psychology to understand us both. And you had that first-hand experience way back in the Bin."

She looked at me as if she'd been hit. The "Bin" was her word for the hospital.

"I'm sorry, Clarissa. It just slipped out. Please, let's make up." I smiled, giving her my most winning look, letting my mask lines go slack. "I'm a dummy. Can you ever forgive me?"

"I don't know." Her lip trembled. "Can you hold me— just hold me and look at me?"

I took a deep breath and kissed her with my eyes wide open.

✠

In cubicle number three we practiced recrimination.

"It's your fault I took seven years to finish my Ph.D.," she said. "Listening to you talk about your boring rocks took at least a year out of my life."

"Only a year?" I asked, and she laughed.

But her laugh reminded me of how things had changed. It was the same laugh I heard these days when she was on the phone and I'd be chipping away at specimens with my hammer in the basement, lighting the Bunsen burner, pounding crystals on my charcoal block, inserting my blowpipe into the edge of the flame.

In addition to working at the Counseling Center, Clarissa was starting a real estate practice and volunteering to do fundraising for the United Way. Whenever we talked, what I heard her really saying was, "Hurry up. I only have so much time." I could tell when she was calling up a man because her voice got hushed and confidential. Chuckling in a controlled, husky tone, she'd say, "You're going to kill me when you hear what it is this time." Maybe the Way needed a Santa suit from the Moose Lodge or some letterhead printed by her friend at Alabama-Northern. Chipping at specimens, I'd think, What is your need, Clarissa? What's your secret need? When she was about to hang up, I'd hear her saying slowly, "Aw, thanks," in this golly, gee-whiz way, her voice toppling end over end.

In number three Clarissa said, "I've invested so much in this relationship. I don't have much more to give."

"I love you, Clarissa."

"This sure is a strange place," she said.

"Good old number three," I said evenly.

This was where we fought; number one was where we made up. I knew Clarissa looked at our meetings as a sort of sacred job, working things through. Me, I liked coming to the vault. I wasn't sure why.

"It's weird." She pursed her lips as if she knew what number one meant to me. "You think if we hauled our buns right over to number one and went at it, everything would be okay? Well, it wouldn't. Alton, I want us to grow together. I'm growing every day, getting stronger and more self-validating. I don't have time for all this...crap."

I didn't know what she meant by "growing." If there was one thing I knew I didn't know how to do, it was grow. Oh, I'd grown physically, but I'd always been me, Alton. Shale, I knew, could metamorphose into slate; granite could turn into banded gneiss. But not me.

"Alton, it's just become too hard."

She closed her ring in my fist and walked out the door, and that had been where we left things.

✢

Now in number one, I couldn't argue with the fact that Clarissa and I had broken up three times in number three and gotten back together only twice in good old number one. This time I wanted the truth. I wouldn't try to kiss her or hold her or cajole her back to me. I was going to divide up our life together, put our meetings in number one and number three into the past.

I spun my ring on my finger. My forehead was hot. Oh, Eloise, I thought, where in the hell am I going from here? The truth, or I should say Clarissa, was knocking at number one.

I opened the door, and she stood there, wearing a gray silk scarf knotted above a black sweater and white skirt. Her face was pale; her dark, straight hair was parted in the middle, a new style. The space between the scarf and the top of her breasts looked porous. Tentatively, as if she were ice that would melt or break, I reached out and pressed the flat of my palm onto the space above her collarbone.

"Your skin's so cool," I said.

She said, "Let's talk."

FIVE

She tugged my hand away and then let go, gazing at me as if from far away. She still wore the obsidian disk I'd cut for her and also the snake heads, but not our white gold.

"Can I come in, please, Alton?" She sneaked a glance at Mr. Vault who rubbed his forehead as if he were speculating on our prospects. "Please, Alton?" she asked, her voice rising.

I nodded and stepped away from her. My throat was burning, as if I'd sucked in flame through my blowpipe.

She closed the door, a hint of a wry smile on her face. It was as if we were back in her attic world. Except here there were no cases of amber and crystal, no skylight, no windows, no bay outside to soften the light on the white walls. Clarissa and I were the two surviving icons from that world, huddled under the orange ceiling light. When she spoke, her voice was cool, white, made of wool or silk, holding our world, protecting it.

"I'm sorry you had to find out like that, Alton."

"Me too." I rested my hands on the Formica counter behind me.

She glanced down at our deposit box, which held her wedding ring. Her white, rough-fibered wool skirt glinted as if it could cut me. Her eyes were soft as the gray water of the bay, setting a bare stage, just as the bay and the islands had been an ever-shifting but constant backdrop to our lives.

I thought of a time we'd climbed to the Larrabee Lookout Point, not long after Clarissa left the hospital. The wooden railing by the drop-off was a bit askew, pushed out, as if people had been leaning against it as they stared out at the islands.

Clarissa had climbed up on the rickety railing and sat dangling her legs over the side, swinging one ankle languidly over the drop-off.

"Do you have to do that?" I asked. "You're making me nervous."

"Don't worry, Alton," she said, bobbing her leg, "I didn't come back from the dead to die falling off a stupid fence."

I took a few child-steps closer, staying an arm's length away. I was scared. I thought that if I took another step, I'd reach out and tip her over the flimsy railing, watching her body bounce down the two-hundred-foot slope of sandstone and gravel, all the way down to the bay. I'd go running back to town shouting, "I murdered my wife, and we're not even married yet."

☨

Now in our white cubicle, Clarissa started to say something but instead just leaned back against the door.

"What were you going to say?" I asked.

"What were *you*?"

She laughed and, unhooking her cream-colored shoulder bag, she set it on the counter by our deposit box.

"I don't want us to hate each other." She turned back to me. "I was going to tell you, Alton. I just didn't want to hurt you."

"You didn't want to *hurt* me," I said, expelling my words like air through my blowpipe.

"Yes, I was protecting you," she shot back, her eyebrows going up, her eyes big. Then she said sadly, "You've always thought you're so reasonable, I didn't have the heart...." She shrugged.

I wondered what she was protecting me from now. What I really wanted was to see how my world had changed, see it like the color change I watched for when testing specimens in flame. I wanted to see what our world had been, what I was losing, what I had lost.

"I've tried to help you, Alton. I'd like to help you now."

"You sound very clinical." I clenched my fist.

"That's correct."

The ventilators whirred; the baseboard heater ticked lightly. The walls of number one had tightened, as if her attic world had contracted to this closet, this stall, this cubicle, and we were two inmates searching for a relic to protect us. The bare, white walls of number one, roughed over in a jagged stucco, had a scratchy texture that caught tiny knots of shadow from the ceiling light and twisted them into something substantial.

"I want to know how it happened," I said.

"Maybe you'll just have to accept it," she said wryly and precisely, sure of what she could offer, that and no more.

☦

I wanted to walk out of this terrible cubicle with her right now—even if it meant giving up on finding Eloise, going back to lecturing about my view of the ages, and even if it meant not knowing what Clarissa's and my world had been.

"How could you? And *Stevens*—all those years."

"Well, it wasn't like I got out of bed every night after you fell asleep. It only happened a few times a year. When he published an article, or when I had to get out."

"When he published articles?" I didn't get it.

"I was trying to keep what we had, Alton—you and me." She sounded angry, yet pleading. "Four or five times a year, that's only, what, seventy or eighty times in sixteen years? I wasn't just doing it for myself."

"What *were* you to each other?"

Again that wry smile, and she tightened the three scar-like lines at the corner of her mouth, just as she'd done as we walked down that white hospital corridor sixteen years ago and she prated grotesquely, "I feel dead, I feel dead."

Now she gave me a gaping, hurt look and said triumphantly, "I've loved you. You must believe that. You can't believe I did this for myself. And not just for Stevens, either."

"Then why?"

She laughed bitterly, the tendons in her neck straining. "To keep us together, Alton. You and me. *We* were what was important. It was either go with him or—"

"Or what?"

Her eyes got big. "It was either that or have a little accident on that fence by the lookout on Larrabee."

"Oh, Clarissa, no."

I had to look away. She'd always talked about her clients acting out and making suicidal gestures as if she were talking about a race of beings different from herself.

Softly, she said, "Alton, look at me. Tell me, do you hate me? Tell me the truth. Tell me."

"I don't hate you, Clarissa."

For a second, I saw Eloise sitting by herself on the curb on Commercial Street with her shoes off.

"Eloise," I cried, "how can you let this happen to me?"

Gently, Clarissa said, "Who's Eloise? Don't tell me you've been unfaithful, too?" She sounded almost relieved.

"Yes, I have," I lied, shouting. "She's not like you. Though she's slept with lots of men—some of them good choices, some of them bad—she's stayed unsullied by it."

"Not like me?" She twisted her mouth until those little lines looked like hooks reeling in all the things she couldn't help, not in herself or in me. "Alton, I'm going to do you a favor. You want the truth—I'm going to give it to you. You want to hear about it? Our first time together, your famous mentor and me?" She came closer so we were almost touching.

How ethereal she was, blue-shadowed, like shapes in snow or ice. Her collarbone, that bare place below her throat, was a thin conduit, lonely and cold. Her fullness made such places look even more frail. One strand of a fine, silver necklace hung below her throat, and another strand hung above her breasts.

"It's not a very inspiring story, Alton. You want to hear it?" she asked, smiling. Her big, mobile mouth had these poor, woeful hooks.

"After we finished, he got up and smoked a cigarette. He held up his hand and blew the smoke through his fingers. God, it made me feel like I was nothing to him. 'Come back to bed,' I said. He said he was going to finish his cigarette. 'You don't care about me,' I said. He just put his cigarette out and lit another one. You weren't ever insensitive like that, Alton."

She twisted her mouth, started to say something, then seemed to change her mind. "I want to show you something. My things, they're here in the vault."

Her face was shy and confiding. Damned if I didn't want to see her things one last time. A knot in my stomach tightened, and a pressure threatened to tear my breastbone down the center.

But I nodded.

☦

She left number one, and in a minute she was back, closing the door behind her and setting down three thin boxes and one tall box fat as a toolbox. Sliding off the steel lids, she drew out her butterscotch amber necklace, the black amber with the pendant carved rose, and the black strand of Peking glass beads. Stacked on trays of purple velvet and protected by velvet partitions, her collection paraded fully dressed, filling the formica counter with its ostentation precisely arranged and numbered. The delicate bone-and-ivory hands holding roses looked creamy but shrunken, pale and thin.

"Guess how much they're worth," she said in a hushed voice.

I shrugged, and she unloaded a black composition notebook from the bottom of one of the thin boxes. She opened it. There were numbers keyed to more numbers. There were headings indicating the amount paid for each item, its worth year by year, yearly sub-totals for the collections of Victoriana, the unusual pieces, and finally a figure in black ink under the heading, *Current Net Worth*.

Clarissa pointed to the figure shyly and proudly, and I saw it exceeded $600,000.

"How in the world did you do this?"

"Well, I was lucky. My total investment during the term of our marriage was less than one thousand per year. I'm going to be quite comfortable. With this as collateral, I've bought three houses whose rentals cover the payments. I'd like to help you, Alton, if you'll let me. I happen to know your personnel committee's meeting soon to discuss the grounds for your dismissal."

"Dismissal?"

"Yes, I'd like to help you, still, Alton."

Pushing one row of her purple trays toward me, she said, "Take anything you like. How much money *do* you have in the bank, by the way?"

My net worth? I didn't know, but I never had much. Maybe blacking out in Stevens' office before I could put my request for a leave in writing hadn't been such a good idea. Nor had carrying on conversations that others must see as imaginary been very smart, either.

If Eloise were here, she'd say, "Get out of here, Alton."

I stared down at the hands carved of ivory and bone. Behind Clarissa, the knots of shadow in the white walls flickered like things that could hurt me.

"There's so much," I said softly. "How'd you—where'd you get the Peking glass beads?"

"I don't remember."

"What about the ivory hands?"

"A dealer. I don't know who."

"Were you excited when you got them?"

"Yes. No. I don't remember." She shifted her feet. "Take anything."

It was as if we were two pharaohs buried with our wealth, discussing old business.

"If you'd *give* me something you like—" I stammered.

"Take anything." She waved her hand carelessly.

"No, I don't think so."

She pressed her lips together, let her breath out sharply, then shrugged. As if merely changing the subject, she asked sadly, "Do you want to make love one last time?" She leaned against the door, one hand playing with the lock on the door handle, open, then closed.

The hollow under her throat was in shadow. One last time, I thought. Maybe I'd walk out of number one a free man, stride past the gray and silver walls, smile at Mr. Vault and chat about prospects. I'd think philosophically of my meetings in number one and number three. Against the backdrop of geological time, they'd seem like specks. When I went back to our house, I wouldn't look out at her birch tree as I worked on specimens. I'd hunt for Eloise who was free and easy and who didn't have hospital eyes that opened up like the bay.

Clarissa stood next to me, not touching me, and then she did touch me, lightly, on one shoulder.

"This isn't fair, is it?" And she smiled.

☦

I remembered an old dream. I'd been tunneling under the loose, wet sand of a beach, pushing toward an opening where the world would be clear, shiny, and cold. Here it was dark—a warm, comfortable, wet dark—and I hauled myself up as if I were trying to pull myself out of a chimney. The walls of warm earth pushed me onward. When I climbed out onto the bright, cold shore, Clarissa stood in front of me, her raised hand holding a knife. She started to plunge the knife down at me, but I caught her arm and held it, and her arm came right off in my hand.

Now in the vault, she tugged her sweater off over her head. Her breasts were bare. I rested my hands on her cool waist.

"It feels like we're having an affair," I said, in a low, croaking voice.

Smiling, she took off the two thin, silver strands of her necklace and laid them on the white counter.

"They get in the way." She draped her arms around my neck as if they were laden and heavy. Her face was flushed.

I kissed her tentatively, then fully. Maybe we'd go back home and she'd come down to my basement workroom. Or we'd go up to her attic. If I opened my eyes, I'd see her birch tree lift its thin arms in the cold sunlight by the bay. Later we'd go for a walk—walk for miles, come back late, climb the steps to her attic, and make love as the islands immersed themselves in layers of thin mist.

Mr. Vault's door clanked open, shut. Clarissa pulled me to her, and we kissed. Kneeling on the tile floor, we undressed.

"Are you disillusioned now, Alton?"

I didn't know what I was. The pressure in my chest felt hot and tight. The cold floor was gritty.

I reached out and held Clarissa feebly, as if I'd forgotten what we were doing and my flesh had lost its memory. I seemed to be able to forget other things, too—this white room, Mr. Vault with his keys and his book. And I could forget my life was going to be divided.

The walls of number one, stark as an elevator's, seemed as if they could plummet any minute, or they could lift us from the lap of the everyday, turning us into beings intent on delighting hopes or murdering them. This close room was our flesh, and we'd come here like souls in search of our bodies. If we walked out of this cubicle onto a bright, cold shore, would we love each other or want to hurt each other?

"I'm scared," Clarissa said. "I'd forgotten."

"Me too."

"I feel unreal." Her eyes got big and starey. "When I was in the hospital, I said that. Unreal, unreal."

"Don't talk about it."

"I've *got* to talk about it." She pressed her chin into my chest. "I'd come to the place where they put scared people. I'd never known there were so many of us. It was very enlightening, a democratizing experience." She smiled, twisting her mouth.

We lay down, curling our legs under the counter covered with her velvet trays of jewels, spotlighted cruelly by the ceiling light.

"Do you love me?" I asked, pressing her tight.

"I *have* loved you, Alton."

She kissed me. It was as if her flesh were quicker to forget than mine was. I lay the flat of my palm against her smooth hip, her thigh. Even as I held her, she eluded me, as if she were sand blowing away. I pressed myself against her. Her crotch felt scratchy, full, protuberant, and I pulled along the length of it lightly the way she liked, slowly loosening and pulling. She was wet.

I felt as if we weren't separate then, as if by touching the folds of her vagina I dissolved the layers that separated us. We weren't ourselves now, but flesh with its secrets, that wasn't afraid, that had no power to will or wish, but only to enter and be entered.

"Would you put your ring back on?" I asked.

"No." She glanced away.

I drew back. Raising myself onto my knees, I braced myself against the counter, feeling the sharp, clean edge of the deposit box where her ring still lived its secret life.

Breathing heavily, I drew my hand along the edge of the metal as if it held a weapon or a pledge. I wished I *had* pushed her off the edge of the Larrabee Lookout when I'd had that crazy impulse.

I grabbed her shoulders, wanting to shake her. "You hurt me!" I cried.

Watchful, she sat up straight, leaning stiffly toward me. Slowly, as if choosing her words carefully, she said, "I was a lot older than you when we met, Alton. Forget what our real ages were. You were still a boy."

And then she smiled, still flesh, as if flesh knew that it could smile.

"People can change." Her gray eyes regarded me solemnly. The knots of shadow that had twisted in the white walls now were part of her body.

"Why, Clarissa? Why?"

She shrugged and said wryly, "Sometimes you have to accept things."

She leaned toward me, as if offering something.

"Well, I can't accept it," I cried, holding my head in my hands. Accepting things was her job, wasn't it? Wasn't that what she went through all that therapy for? If she wasn't the oracle of these white walls, who was?

"You have nothing else to say?" I asked.

She sat with her legs curled under her, one hip jutting up. "How you romanticize me, Alton. I'm really very ordinary. I want nice things, these things."

She spoke quietly, her voice not flesh, not wool or silk, not protecting us. Yet she still seemed to offer something. But I'd forgotten why we'd come here and what I'd wanted. And then I remembered. It was cruel to be robbed of her again just when I was about to have her like another first time.

"You don't want to hurt me, do you, Alton?" she asked softly.

I shook my head, and she breathed a deep sigh. I knew I was powerless to change her or help her or make her feel anything, and oddly, I felt relieved. I sat beside her, dazed and still excited, pulling my knees up and resting my head on them. She curled her arm around my neck lightly, in a comradely way.

"It's been a long time, hasn't it, Alton? A long time."

I started crying. I was losing her and going I didn't know where, going to look for Eloise who was what? A fiction. I was going crazy, and I was going to be alone and crazy, and I wasn't going to get to make love to Clarissa like a second first time.

Choking, I pressed my face into her neck, crying for a long time—not a long time on any time scale a geologist is used to—but longer than I thought a man could cry. My eyes were hot and clenched, and I let my tears go on, hungry for this choking closeness.

We weren't flesh now or souls either, but something forced up out of the earth. As Clarissa held me, not saying anything, she seemed to take my pain for the love it was, receiving it, as my choking sounds still fused us. I kept waiting for it to stop, and then it did stop, and I looked at her, feeling emptied, dazed, and still excited.

"Sometimes people cry in anger," she said softly.

"I love you!" I cried.

We held each other awkwardly, propped together like sticks. The tips of her breasts were like the tough, nubbed buds of chestnut trees in spring. We lay down on the cold, tile floor. Her body was cool. Her belly seemed made of ivory or bone, and I moved slowly.

We made love slowly. It was as if I were crawling up a white stone well, her belly. Soon I'd taste her ivory rooms. My bones seemed to move slowly, knowing how alone they were, spreading themselves to meet the walls of this well, waiting, holding themselves ready. Clarissa seemed to know I was going to be able to wait for her. She pulled me to her, forcing me up through her, thrusting and tugging, bumping her pelvic bone against me, meeting my thrusts, until we both collapsed, awed by our cries.

We lay still a long time. When I opened my eyes, Clarissa was disentangling herself from me. I reached out for her.

"We have to go, Alton,"" she said in a controlled way, as she got up and started to dress, her back to me. "They're closing up the bank."

What had been number one now seemed a small, bare room in an out-of-the-way motel. I wished Mr. Vault *would* knock on our door, so we could sign his book and start all over.

Clarissa pulled her black sweater over her head and smoothed it down over her white skirt. I lay still. Behind her, the ivory hands on the counter seemed the price we were going to pay so we could walk out of here.

"Aren't you getting up?" She nudged me with her bare foot. "They'll lock you in, you know."

"I'm staying."

"Okay, suit yourself." She started packing up her velvet trays, stacking the purple layers into their boxes.

If I were going to be alone, I thought, I'd better start practicing. I could live here—catch glimpses of Clarissa when she came here to look at her collection. We'd have something in common. When she came in, I'd stop her and say, "Hi, I'm the elephant that can't forget, but maybe I could learn to forgive." But how was I going to tell her that if I never got up? And I wasn't going to get up. The floor of number one was familiar, close, and cold.

"Take care of yourself, Alton." She smiled and closed the door behind her.

‡

Number one wouldn't be so bad if they really heated it, I thought, and not just with baseboard heat. They should really heat it so I could sink into it like a hot tub—heat it to one hundred forty degrees. Then I'd soak till my bones remembered why I was here or until Eloise hauled me out.

I got up slowly and locked the door. When I took off my ring and put it in our deposit box beside Clarissa's, the box looked very lonely on the white counter. Then I changed my mind, took my ring out, and put it in my pants pocket, first in my left front pocket with my car and house keys, and then transferring it to my right front pocket, which I usually kept empty, and where I'd be less likely to forget it. I might need to hock the thing, I thought.

Someone was rattling the door, probably Mr. Vault. Maybe I should ask him if I could spend the night. Of course, if it were any trouble, I'd go. But what if someone came in the morning and found me sleeping here? It might hurt my chances with the personnel committee, too, if I were found sitting naked in number one. "My wife was here with me," I could tell them.

The knocking came again, and I threw on my clothes, yelling, "Just a minute." When I opened the door, it wasn't Mr. Vault, but Clarissa.

"I forgot," she said, handing me a slip of paper— Counseling Center stationery—with three names and phone numbers scribbled on it. "I wanted to refer you to someone who can—well, this isn't the professional thing to do, but I do care about you, Alton."

I took the piece of paper solemnly, the way she offered it, and we filed out of the vault together, walking past the gray and silver walls, the clanking iron door, and past a silent but dogged-looking Mr. Vault's outpost of new prospects. We stalked down the shiny white corridor, climbed the orange-carpeted stairway, and walked into the late afternoon sunlight on Commercial Street.

"I guess you'll be looking for a new bank, huh?" I said. "There are too many memories here."

"Goodbye, Alton."

✣

I didn't know where to go. I was crying. When I got to my car, I thought about going to the Miracle. No, it was too clean and bright. My place—Clarissa's and my old house— was impossible. So I drove to the beach where Clarissa and I had gone when she first got out of the hospital, the beach where we stared at the big cedar log and she cried and said how far she'd come.

Next to the log lay a flat, round stump, wide as a table top, and I sat down next to it, resting my chin on the stump's rough chin. "It's a rough life," I murmured, wagging my head back and forth on this big chopping block, trying to decide what to do next.

I got up and started walking down the beach, which was covered with a bed of seaweed stiff as turf. The cold, wet carpet stretched as far as I could see, and I scrunched along the edge of the green-and-gray world, thinking how beautiful the water was, how soft and gray. If I walked into it and swam until I was too tired to swim back, how peaceful it would be, sleeping on that green turf. But choking wouldn't be much fun, and how humiliating it'd be if I got out there and then changed my mind. I'd probably start thrashing and swallowing gulps of salt water, yelling for Eloise to save me. And then I wished that Eloise were here, saying, "Yes, you'd be sorry." And I wished I had a better imagination, that I *were* crazy, so I could hear her say something to me.

As I walked down the bright, green shore, I picked up some rocks—porphyritic variety—and started chucking them at the grizzled pilings eaten away by water and covered with barnacles.

"Clarissa's a bitch!" I shouted, and I hit one of the pilings square and felt better. "She's a bitch, she's a bitch," I shouted at the cold, gray islands and the soft water. "Hospital eyes," I shouted, chucking another stone. "One last time!" And I hit another piling and felt good as the wood chips flew out of its side.

I kept throwing rocks till my arm ached, and I scuffed along the green shore, feeling almost confident, ready for anything.

"Eloise!" I shouted at the islands and the gray water. "I'll find you. I'll search for you."

SIX

There wasn't an answer, not from the islands and not from Eloise, either. November turned into December, and the winter rains slid down my thick windows. In the Bluestone Apartments, which I'd moved into the day after my last meeting with Clarissa in the vault, I had two small, furnished rooms connected by glass doors to a big kitchen that looked out on the bay. The Bluestone, a square, two-story building on a block of frame houses three miles west of Clarissa's and my old house, was owned by the woman on Indian Street who'd been repotting her monster—Miss Bosom, I called her.

From here the islands seemed bigger. The bay was a gray lake, and the purple islands closed it in. I lived in deep time, geological time, the blameless stretches of four billion years. On December 6th, I recorded the following facts in my diary: 1) Clarissa and I were finished; 2) I'd been screwed; 3) I didn't care if I taught my classes or not; 4) my payroll check hadn't arrived on November 15th, nor had one arrived on the 30th; 5) my bank balance was $428.66; 6) a letter had come from Stevens, postmarked November 18th, but I hadn't opened it. I used it for a bookmark.

In the Bluestone, I slept roughly three hours a night. On my seventh day there, I woke from a long sleep filled with dreams. Eloise had told me to put my arm around Clarissa's waist, and I did it. I woke up. For breakfast I ate eggs and bacon, toast, and tea with lots of honey. As I stared over the wet roofs, a crow lit on the tilted, swaying top of a hemlock.

The rains fell, and the hills steamed, as if fires had smoldered for centuries in wet earth that couldn't quench the flames. In the arboretum near campus, the forest of hemlock and Douglas fir rose, rank and profuse. Clumps of swordferns glistened, good fodder for my old friends, Brontosaurus and Stegosaurus, whom I'd read about in my dinosaur books as a child. I couldn't see the mountains; they were out of focus. Sky and earth coalesced. Or rather, the sky held the earth in its misty clasp.

One night I dreamt I climbed Mount Baker. I leaped crevasses and crept under cornices of ice. Smoke sifted out of a vertical slot the shape of a half-moon. I wrapped my arms around the smoke. My throat burned as the mountain collapsed out from under me. I rode a dense, white wave, sliding slowly. "Eloise," I cried. She waved goodbye.

I didn't teach, didn't go to my office, didn't answer the phone. Nor did I call Emily. I wrote a brief note to my parents, telling them the fact was I couldn't write them this month. Each day I lugged my laundry bag to the Miracle, reading and rereading the stories. Then I staked out Employment Security, the junk shops in Old Town, and the sewage treatment plant at Marine Park.

In my diary, I wrote letters to Clarissa I never sent. One started, "I'm writing on one of the few days that hasn't seemed awful." I started another, simply, "Screw you, Clarissa. I feel craven and cloying, and I don't care what you think about it." I didn't send that one either. Another doozy was this one: "I never loved you, Clarissa—not your eyes, not your thin arms, not the blue veins on the inside of your wrists."

According to my diary, I thought of Eloise 6,027 times per day, as compared to 428 for Clarissa, 367 for Stevens, and, I confess, a measly 111 for Emily. At the Miracle, I reread the stories in *Yes, I Don't Love You*. Sometimes I went out into the parking lot and did jumping jacks. Cars hummed up and down the freeway overpass, their steady murmur reminding me of binding vows.

My favorite stories weren't the outrageous ones—not "Looking," in which Eloise carries her saddle on subways in New York as she hunts for an apartment; not "I Want You (With Apologies to B.D.)," in which Eloise writes love letters to Bob Dylan and tries to imitate his singing voice; not "Confessions of a Teenage Librarian," in which Eloise works part-time in her college library and, through a poignant misunderstanding, becomes a double agent for the FBI and the Vegetarian League.

In "The Gecko," she smokes a cigar-like joint of ganja in Kingston, Jamaica, with the Rastafarians, who hold a religious ceremony in a suburban home and pray to Haile Selassie to destroy the Whore of Babylon, i.e., America. Lying sprawled on a couch, bonkered on ganja, she examines her lizard suction cups. That episode was also too dark for me at that time.

I did like the stories that, as the jacket copy says, "travel the continent and delve into some risky inner country, too." I liked Eloise saying, "I didn't see the *Adventures in Paradise* side of Hawaii, but it was a kick." I also liked some of the stirring passages from the "On the Road" stories. Witness this upliftingly offbeat musing of hers: "Glimpses of wheat fields go by. Why only glimpses? Guess I get bored looking at all that goddamn wheat."

☩

On wet November afternoons, sometimes I ran into a man I called Mr. Nostalgia.

"Hi," he'd say sadly, materializing from behind a drooping cedar in Elizabeth Street Park. "Do you theenk this rain, eet will stop?"

He was a frail man in his forties with a Spanish accent. His face, a wispy mixture of Asian and American Indian features, was made of dark slabs that had become interbedded.

"Sure," I said, "it'll stop." I liked the hopeful sound of the word "sure."

"Tchoor," he agreed sadly. "But these clouds, they are a nostalgia, no?" He spoke gently, tenuously, nodding weakly, as if the envelope of his flesh might collapse if I disagreed.

"It's getting closer to spring," I said.

"Ees a nostalgia," he repeated, nodding dreamily, his eyes filmy as milk glass.

I smiled, thinking of a friend's sad smile. I kicked a stone and turned onto Holly Street. A crow that had been following me divebombed past my ear and landed on my shoulder, clacking its beak at me.

"Do *you* know where Eloise is?" I asked.

☦

When I went in the Salvation Army Thrift Store, the place smelled of mildew and old clothes. A young woman in a denim jacket stood by a rack of blouses. She jerked at the arm of her toddler who was picking at a loose piece of linoleum.

"Cut it out," she shouted, "or I'll take you up to Mount Baker and feed you to the wolves and bears."

"You know her, don't you?" I cried, for a second back in my dream, up on Baker.

Frowning, the woman marched her son downstairs, swinging him in the air as they vanished into the basement.

"Eloise, Eloise," I muttered.

The clerk at the register glanced at me. Above him, in a huge oil painting, a horse with gauzy eyes lunged into moonlit waves. Shaking, I sorted through a dog-eared stack of records—the Cowsills, *The Rites of Spring*. The Cowsills? Back in the Sixties, I used to dance around our living room to that song about the rain and the flower girl, until one day Clarissa pronounced the song "dipshit."

Now as I pressed the album to my lips, a drawing of three women slipped out of the record jacket. One of the women was Emily; one was Eloise. A crow sat on her shoulder. The artist's signature was a messy scrawl.

I rolled up the drawing and ran out of the store.

✝

It was windy, drizzling lightly, as I turned the corner of Diamond Street and pulled the Valiant over. Gray-white smoke from the Alabama-Northern mill spilled over the bay. A tall, thin woman was heading toward the alley. Her back to me, she carried a big cardboard box.

I got out and started running. "Emily!"

The wind rushed through the big double spruce tree, and I slowed to a galumphing walk. When she turned, I tried to give her my Rock of Ages grin, but my face felt stuck.

She shifted the box in her arms. "Alton, I've been calling you and calling you."

That sweetly accusing tone of voice—a ping echoed in my chest. I reached out to help her and saw the box was filled with typewritten pages. She hugged it closer, frowning. On the topmost page was the word, "Eloise."

"What's this?" I cried, bending over, clutching the cardboard flaps of the box.

Emily picked that moment to let go. The box slipped, fell through my hands, bounced off my foot, and tipped over. The wind swirled the pages down the street.

She laughed a strange laugh, half an indignant wail, as

if she were doing battle with forces out of her control. She raced after a dervish-like whirl of white paper. I picked up a chunk of banded gneiss, probably a glacial erratic, and stuck it on top of the stack of billowing pages.

"Shit, shit, Alton—" she was calling me to attention— "help me."

The wind blew us down the darkening street as we bent and snatched at pages. Kneeling, we stuffed them under the banded gneiss. Our hands bumped, and the streetlights came on. The small porches of frame houses eyed me disconsolately.

"I'm sorry, Emily," I said. I meant, sorry if I'd made her lose her pages, sorry I hadn't written her.

She peered at me, eyes bright, hair blowing. She pursed her lips in a kind of harrumph. "Alton, I've been worried. Where have you been?"

✠

Emily's apartment, a converted attic, was all corners and angles, ceiling meeting the walls at eye level. Dormer windows faced the bay. Wall hangings in orange, rust, and brown decorated the cream-colored walls. There were posters of leaves labeled by name and family. Hanging plants draped down in front of the windows. Her desk, a broad oak door laid across two filing cabinets, was bare except for her typewriter, a stack of white bond paper, and a box of crayons. In her bookcase stood maybe forty copies of *Yes, I Don't Love You, Merlin*.

After we'd put the pages back in their box, Emily had lugged it to a garbage can in the alley, dumped the box in, and set the lid on the can with a clatter. She hadn't let me look at one page.

She sat erect on a tattered blue sofa under a dormer window. She sipped tea, sometimes glancing nervously behind her out the window. The lights of the boat harbor and the billowing pulp mill glimmered. On her aging stereo, harps and penny whistles, liquid and piercing, played a song that reminded me of summer.

"Are you back so I can stick you in a story, Alton?" Emily asked, jutting out her small, sharp chin.

"No." My mug of tea was warm in my hands.

"You said you'd call."

I frowned, glancing at her books. "I'd said I'd write, not call."

Emily sighed, said angrily, "I guess you've been spending lots of time with *her.*"

"No, my wife and I—"

"Oh, you're so dense. I meant your Eloise." She set her lips in a thin line, her dark hair still wild.

What did she mean, *my* Eloise?

"No, I haven't found her." I fiddled with my briefcase, which held the drawing of the three women.

"So you've been scrounging around, being a regular Magnum, P.I.?"

I hung my head. I hadn't asked questions. What a dummy I was.

"You've been sulking, haven't you, Alton?" she said playfully, smiling up at me. "Oh, I knew it. After that slick, young T.A. took over your class, we missed your digressions about.... Maybe you should go back to your wife, Alton," she said kindly in her clipped voice.

I told her about Clarissa and Stevens. Emily shook her head, trying not to, but smiling her one-sided smile. "I could've told you, Alton," she said sadly, then glanced back over her shoulder.

Told me what? Maybe everyone in town knew about me and the vault. Damn, this wasn't the story I had in mind.

"But Eloise, now she's gone, too. Can't I even keep one of those pages?"

She shook her head and smiled. "You know, Alton, it's just like her, to leave you in the lurch like that."

I glanced away. On her desk, the box of crayons, 128

colors, weren't what I'd expected. Following my look, she said ruefully, "I've stopped writing, Alton. I like to doodle. I'm much happier now." Her voice had a strange gaiety.

"You'll feel like writing again," I said.

"I told you, I haven't written a thing in six months." She sounded definite—even a bit impatient. She pushed back her hair, crossed and recrossed her legs.

"But Emily, what were those pages?"

She gave me an edgy laugh. "First drafts."

"But drafts of the...*stories?*"

"I forgot I had them." There was something playful yet guilty in her voice.

"Why'd you want them back," I asked, "just to throw them out?"

She made that waving motion with one hand. "Stop giving me the third degree, Alton. When something's over, I want it over. I'm a terrible packrat. That's what Meg always said." She shrugged, frowning as if I should know this.

"Who's Meg?"

"She was my sister." She gestured in a vague way toward a framed, color, five-by-seven photo on the wall above her desk.

I got up. In the snapshot, three women sat on a grassy hillside. One of them was Eloise.

"That's her!" I cried.

The three women squinted into bright sunlight. Eloise wore a red headband and looked happy. No crow sat on her shoulder. Emily looked younger and happier, too.

"Meg died thirteen years ago," said Emily sadly, her green-brown eyes shining, dark at the edges. "In Saigon," she added, frowning, as she stared at me intently.

In her clipped voice, she told me Meg had been a reporter for an underground newspaper, *Passages*. Her body had been shipped back to Sehome and buried here. Emily bowed her head, clasping her hands behind her neck. "We never even got to say goodbye, Alton."

"But that's Eloise." It wasn't fair for Emily to tell me she was someone else.

Scowling, she got up and started pacing. She paused, gave me a pleading look, and said my name softly.

Slowly, I went over, opened my briefcase, and lifted out the sketch of the three women. When I handed it over, Emily took my gift gravely with both hands.

"Where'd you *get* this?" she gasped.

I told her, and she sat down, eyes wet and tinged with wonder. Shuddering, she let out a rich, sad laugh, as if at a joke she didn't find entirely funny.

"Alton, look, it says 'AP.' It's an artist's proof."

And she was crying. "Alton, we thought it was lost. There was this fire. At my folks' place, on March Point Road." She wiped her eyes precisely, first one eye, then the other.

When I sat down next to her on the sofa, she touched my hand. "She's haunting us both then, Alton."

"You've seen her?"

"I saw someone."

"Where?"

"On Holly."

"Near the Salvation Army?"

Emily glanced away, pursing her lips. For a second, she didn't answer, but then in a flat tone, she said, "If you must know, it was past the scrap metal place. In Old Town. Near the old SDS storefront, where she used to work. If you want to call it work."

She laughed a thin laugh.

"I even went to a detective, Alton, just to make sure." She sounded angry at herself. "Nada. No dice."

So, she'd hired the Magnum, P.I., and come up empty. I drew back my hand and, pointing to the older woman in the photo, I asked, "Who's she?"

"That's my mother."

"Who took the picture?"

"My father. That's him, the one who's never there."

✝

Something thudded against a window. Emily turned and shouted, "Alton!" She got up, eyes wide with fear.

I caught a glimpse of someone on the landing. I ran to the window, threw it open.

"Don't go out there," cried Emily, one hand on my shoulder.

But I climbed out, and she clambered out with me. We rattled down rickety wooden steps, ran past a dying garden out to her alley. Nothing. We ran around front, but the street was empty, too. In the mild chinook wind, the double spruce tree heaved and swayed, and a big yellow half-moon hung over the housetops at the top of Sehome Hill.

"Was it *her*?" I asked.

Emily shook her head, lips trembling. Then she touched my arm. "It was a man I don't ever want to see. I based Dink Merlin on him. His looks, I mean. I wrote letters to this prison inmate. In Monroe? I know he's locked up, but still—" She gave a brittle laugh, then glared.

We went around back and stood by a dying garden that hadn't been turned under. The half-moon was going down.

"That wind's really something," I said.

"It feels like spring," Emily said in a poignant, musical way and bowed her head. "Would you stay the night, please? I'm scared. You can sleep on my couch." Her voice was low, shy yet insistent. Our shoulders brushed.

"I'll stand guard out here," I offered, moving away. I didn't think Eloise would approve.

"Oh, you're impossible, Alton." She laughed her rich, sad laugh, but she took my hand.

The mild wind rushing through the big trees seemed to move through my bones, telling me I'd been cold a long time. Over the housetops, the wobbly half-moon had a greenish tinge at the edges. I wanted to hold Emily, but I felt disloyal.

As if in a shadowy procession, we filed toward Emily's front door. The double spruce, I saw, was two separate trees whose trunks had become intertwined. Slowly, we went upstairs.

SEVEN

As I stood by the desk under the snapshot of the three women, sounds of hangers clattering and clothes rustling came from behind Emily's bedroom door. On the living-room couch, she'd piled sheets and blankets, but I couldn't believe they were for me, a man who hadn't made it into her story. That damnable Dink we'd glimpsed on the landing—even he had more rights here than I did.

Her bedsprings creaked, light glowing under her door. I turned to the photo, comparing it with the artist's proof. In the five-by-seven glossy, the women had dimension, life. In the flat, black-and-white sketch, they gazed in different directions. Eloise's crow was my crow.

Emily's door opened, and she stood there, pale and expectant. Her dark hair shone. Just above the collar of her high-necked, purple bathrobe, a scar showed, running up one side of her neck.

"Goodnight, Alton?" she asked softly, frowning, pulling her collar up.

"Goodnight," I said, and her door closed.

The rows of her story collection on the bookshelf rebuked me. Wide awake, I went to the kitchen window. Smoke from the pulp mill blew across the floating lights of the boat harbor. In this house with its odd corners and angles, I was floating, too. Out in the alley, the garbage can stood its silent guard. I'll just have a look at those pages, I thought.

I snuck downstairs, went around the back. Softly lifting the box of pages from the trash can, I lugged it to the Valiant. Under the dome light, I read the following: "Eloise vacuumed...." A car's brakes screeched. A garbage can lid clattered as the wind turned it end-over-end down the street. *What if the Dink came back?*

I doused the light, stashed the pages in my trunk, and crept upstairs.

‡

In the morning when I dragged myself off the couch, Emily was in the kitchen, sopping up a mess of black coffee that had spilled over the edge of the counter.

"I forgot to put the pot under the damn thing," she said, circles under her eyes.

She wore a blue turtleneck and a black skirt that went down to dark boots. In her rapid-fire way, she said she had a class to teach at eleven and a doctor's appointment in the afternoon—just a check-up—and she'd called her Magnum, P.I., a man named Wes Nevitt, who said her convict was still locked up.

"Are you okay?" I asked, standing beside her, my head aching. I'd slept a few hours toward dawn.

"Yes, Alton." She sounded edgy. "You can get cups, you know."

I got them. Framed by the window, she poured coffee from a freshly-made pot. Behind her, sunlight glinted on dry cornstalks and the empty garbage can lying on its side in the alley.

She sat down at a red kitchen table that had an old cigarette burn. Above her on a piece of corkboard hung the drawing of the three women. I sat down, too, opened *Yes, I Don't Love*

You to the part in "Confessions" where the Dink, alias Phil Slaymaker, alias Merlin, hatched his kidnap plans.

"I love how you put that, Emily." Thinking of the man I'd seen with Eloise outside the Salvation Army Thrift Store, I read aloud, "'his square, boyish face and his up-river, arrogant smile.' That's so accurate."

Emily frowned, bunching her dark eyebrows up. "I'd rather not discuss it," she said in a flat tone.

"But aren't you scared he'll come back?"

"It was nothing, Alton, just my imagination." Damn, she didn't even say "our" imaginations.

Nettled, I read on: "In that house on Enterprise Road, with its yard full of trucks and weeds, piles of fish net, waifs and bruisers came and—"

"Stop it, Alton. I'm not in the mood."

I didn't stop.

"'The Dink traded motorcycles and beat-up Chevy Novas. He came back from Canada with lots of bucks. His favorite expressions were "Bomb it" and "Bring the war home." Maybe it's time, she thought. She'd always been the one to leave.'"

Emily snatched her book out of my hands.

"How could you give her a creep like that for a lover?" I asked.

Emily shook her head, smiled sadly.

"But you said you based his looks on your convict."

"He's not *my* convict. And I write fiction. I just don't change some things. Faces or real places. It's not cheating. It's just, I don't know, less confusing that way. But they're fictional, Alton. I'm using them fictionally."

Her dark eyes were intent. I glanced down.

"Are you disappointed?" she asked with an odd, expectant smile.

"No, but that Dink Merlin, he's so—" Well, unreasonable. "And Eloise, she doesn't need him. She has me now."

Emily stuck out her small chin. "Are you telling me what

to write? My non-husband used to try and do that. He didn't like my writing about him one bit." Her laugh had a bite to it. "He said I turn people into something unreal."

I shivered. "Your *non*-husband? Have you been apart?"

"What we were was apart. Ma Bell, the great mediator and moderator." As she waved her hand with a sort of noblesse oblige, my knees felt weak. In her staccato voice, she explained how she'd left New York to take the position of visiting writer here at North Cascades.

"East-west, cross-continental. Two years, and I'm still visiting. They'll never ask me to stay." Her voice rose. "Alton, he's got this drinking problem. And he likes drugs. And he hates the Northwest. And he doesn't believe in getting married. I don't give a shit anymore."

She gave a flat laugh. "So it's over. Big deal. I left him. That's me. I'm always the one to—" She paused, tilted her cup, and frowning, set it down with a clatter.

Always the one to leave? But that was Eloise. It hurt me how Emily talked about herself in her pained, self-mocking way.

Scowling, she curled one hand under the top of her turtleneck where her scar would be.

"What is that thing on your neck, Emily, if you don't mind my asking?" The words slipped out, my voice too loud.

She made a face. "It's a cyst. Sebaceous. I had it removed that week I saw you. Not to worry." She got up and went to the window. "I should turn those damn things under," she said angrily. Her voice turned wistful. "They picked up the garbage, huh?"

I nodded and decided to take my plunge.

"Will you help me look for her, Emily?" I asked. "Show me the real places you wrote about in the stories?"

Sighing, she held up her hands, as if to say she'd hired the Magnum, P.I., and what else should she do. "Spirits are supposed to come looking for you, aren't they, Alton?" she said ruefully, precisely.

"I thought you didn't believe in them," I said.

"I don't, but *she* did. When we were kids, Meg had this poltergeist. She called him—" Emily paused, smiling painfully. "She called him Merlin. Said he put Dad's cigar butts in the refrigerator and pipe stems in the cat's ears. And things were always breaking. Then it stopped. I guess we grew up. Now it's crazy, but I keep dropping things. Or breaking them, or losing them." She frowned at me as if it were my fault.

"Are you sure your sister died?"

"We saw the body." She sounded pained, impatient. "Look, Nevitt even talked to her old friends. She didn't have many by the end."

She laughed bitterly. I frowned.

"Oh, I forgot, to you she's the wonderful Eloise." She sighed, glanced at her watch, and got up. "Look, I've got to go now." Turning, she asked, "What are you going to do?"

I shrugged. Maybe hit the Miracle. For sure have a look at those pages I'd stashed away. What if Eloise saw them, the real sides of her Emily had rejected?

"I meant, what about your job, Alton?"

Right, there was that letter from Stevens, but she didn't have to keep changing the subject on me.

"Maybe you should get your retirement benefits out. Can you do that? I don't know. I'm just part-time." She paused. "But I've got this student who works as a watchman. At a warehouse? They let him bring his typewriter. Maybe you could work there, too."

"But I'm not writing a novel."

"Maybe you're living one." She laughed as she snatched up her book from the table and strode off toward her bedroom.

The forty copies of *Yes, I Don't Love You* seemed to stand between me and my real life.

"How come you have so many copies?" I gestured toward her books.

"They were remaindered, for God sake. I bought them back for a dollar apiece. Fame. The fruits of labor." She tossed off her words in a bright, mocking way, as she smiled her lopsided smile.

"Can I come to your class with you?"

"No, Alton." She made that waving, qualifying gesture. "But my class and I, we're giving a reading next week. You can come to that. Now I've got to go."

"I'll stand guard again tonight," I offered.

"That's not necessary." She went into her bedroom. Drawers banged, a door slammed, and in a minute, she came out. Behind her, drawers yanked from her dresser lay on her bed, hangers and clothes strewn across them.

She was crying. "Alton, my jacket's gone. It's missing. *She* gave it to me. It was the only thing of hers I had left. I think I'm losing my fucking mind."

✝

Back at the Bluestone, I spread out Emily's rough drafts on my faded carpet like a jumble of contorted rock facies. I knew about angular unconformities, whole layers eroded from the rock record. As I compared the drafts to her finished versions, I found page after page Emily had recopied with minor variations, as if she couldn't go on until each page was perfect.

Then I came to a part that wasn't in *Yes, I Don't Love You*. The handwriting was a scribble, almost like Eloise's:

> They wired shut the head librarian's office with extension cords. They piled chairs in hallways, brought in sandwiches through windows. They moistened handkerchiefs and tied them around their mouths, stacked blankets to wrap the tear gas canisters.
>
> It was the fifth day. The bust hadn't come. Sun poured in the windows, and the Dink got out a vacuum cleaner. She damn well wasn't doing any vacuuming. She was sick. The

edema made her body retain water so she felt bloated. Someone had put the Youngbloods on the stereo, and she hummed along: something about love and a song and the way people die. There's other ways, she thought.

Oh, no, she was sick. I turned the page over:

Big deal, they had the freaking Secretary of Agriculture. The Dink was a Dink. In the house on Enterprise Road, she waited for her guardian angel, the one who'd make her well. As Eloise vacuumed the mauve throw rug they got at the Salvation Army, she muttered, "Bomb the whole fucking thing."

Oh, my God, she's vacuuming. Eloise really is sick. I ran downstairs, drove out to Enterprise Road, taking the back way through Old Town on Marine Drive toward Gooseberry Point. The blue-white peaks of the Canadian Coastal Range shimmered. Near the Lummi Reservation, I turned north, went roaring past the chain-link-fenced refineries of Ferndale, then chugged slowly down the length of Enterprise Road. But I found no brown house with trucks and motorcycles in the yard.

As I headed back to town on the freeway, the snow dome of Mount Baker floated over the wet brown fields. I pulled the Valiant over at the Miracle where the blue and red pipes painted onto the walls gleamed under the fluorescent lights.

A young woman in a denim jacket stood behind the counter, holding a blue coat swathed in plastic. She was the woman in the Salvation Army Store who'd threatened to leave her kid up on Mount Baker.

"Do you know her?" I cried out. "Eloise. She sent me a postcard from here."

Swiftly pulling the end of a hanger out of a hole in the plastic, she gave me a blank look.

"Do you know her?" I pounded my fist on the counter.

The woman went over to a wall phone, punched some

numbers, and asked to speak to the desk sergeant. I backed away.

✝

At Employment Security, I hung around by the job board. Still no sign of Eloise. None at the 7-Eleven, either, where she had bragged about her friend Merlin, alias the Dink. I got back in the Valiant and drove south past Boulevard Park and its huge beached log. At Larrabee Park, I climbed to the lookout where Clarissa and I had gone when she got out of the hospital. I gazed at the cold, gray islands.

I drove northeast on the Mount Baker highway into the dark first- and second-growth forest under a low gray sky. Near the snow line, I stopped and put chains on my tires, then climbed in first gear past ledges of columnar basalt, cliffs of contorted schists, and misty chasms that beckoned. I tried not to think of facts such as the lack of a guardrail on this icy road.

"Eloise!" I shouted into the fog and snow.

The Juan de Fuca Plate, I knew, was butting the mountain up, a few centimeters a year. Me, I was getting nowhere.

Back in town on Commercial Street, I chatted with Mr. Vault. Clarissa had been in once, he said. When he offered to let me dust off the valuables, I declined.

The next morning, I called Emily. I had stood my guard outside her house but saw nothing. When I asked about her check-up, she said it had been routine. In an edgy, sad yet expectant way, she asked, "You haven't seen her, have you?" I thought of the first time she called me on the phone, when she'd been just a voice—wistful, familiar, accusing.

Then she softened. "Alton, my parents called. My niece, her name's Meg, too. Well, she's staying with them over the holidays." She paused. "My folks want to help me buy a house. It's a fixer-upper, the one on Enterprise Road. I lived there once. With her. I don't know, Alton." She sighed. "Do you want to go look at a house?

✝

That afternoon, we sat once again in her kitchen. First we had gone to the *Passages* office where the old SDS storefront used to be. The Lighthouse Mission next door eyed me disconsolately. When Emily asked curtly if anyone knew Meg Weed, a huge, balding man with big arms glanced up from a table where he'd been stuffing envelopes.

"Have you seen her?" I asked.

"Hey, man, you like to spend your time hunting for dead people?"

Emily turned on her heel. "Hippie arrogance" had been her one comment as we drove back to her place.

Now my friend and I sat under the drawing of the three women. If anything, Eloise seemed farther away than ever.

"What things did you base on your sister?" I asked.

"Well, her looks for one thing. When we were kids, people said we looked alike. I never thought so." Emily got up and went over to the window, frowning. I got up, too.

"What's that stuff about bombed cars and the FBI and people following her?" I asked. "And why's her friend the Dink always in Canada? Is he smuggling something? Drugs?"

Shrugging, she laughed. "Slow down, Alton. Meg had some pretty strange friends."

"But what about that ape-like guy, Caesar?"

"Oh, he's a sweetie, really. He lived downstairs when we shared a place on Carolina Street. Near the motorcycle store? He used to scare me at first. I was too chicken to go down and ask them to turn down the noise, but Meg would go down, and in five minutes it'd be quiet." Emily laughed. "Of course, she might not get home that same night."

Eloise isn't promiscuous, I thought. She's a free spirit.

"But what about her bombed car? And that threat by the League, kidnapping the Secretary?" I shook my head.

Emily smiled an odd smile. Sounding almost nostalgic,

she went on. "Well, Meg did have a car that caught on fire once. She'd parked it in front of the SDS office. Isn't that weird?"

"But what's going to happen to Eloise?" I cried. Emily grinned, her eyelids crinkling at the corners. "That's sweet, Alton, you're worried." Her voice was sad, yet she gazed at me hopefully.

"I am." Why wasn't she worried, too? After all, the Dink said whatever Eloise could do, he could do better.

"Why haven't you been writing, Emily?"

Standing by her counter with its neat row of canisters, its jar of wooden spoons, she looked away out the window at her dead garden. She still hadn't turned it under.

Turning, her hand brushed mine, and she said sadly, "I thought I got Meg out of me, Alton—made her into someone else. I guess not."

‡

It was late afternoon when we pulled off Enterprise Road by a big brown house. All its windows had been knocked out. There was a *FOR SALE* sign lying on top of a heap of fishnet. Emily got out of the Valiant, picked up the sign, and stuck it back into the ground.

We'd driven northwest on the freeway, Mount Baker vague and illusory over the brown fields. When I first came here to teach sixteen years ago, starting my new life on the thin edge of that decade's westward-ho, my parents and the whole country lay back East behind those mountains. But here "back East" meant eastern Washington, the dry side of the state, Stevens had told me.

Emily and I stood beside the Valiant. "When did you and your sister live here?" I asked.

"Before she went away."

A twisted willow tree trailed pale-yellow branches, the sun small and low in the sky. Dry weeds hissed in the wind.

I could smell the river, but I couldn't see it.

"Wasn't there a willow tree in front of the house on March Point Road where Eloise grew up?" I asked.

"No, Alton." Her voice rose, impatient.

"What things *weren't* based on your sister?"

Emily frowned.

"What about fishing in Alaska? Did Meg do that?"

"No." She bent down and picked a dry blade of grass.

"Did she carry a saddle in New York?"

"Of course not."

"Did she get lost in the Metropolitan Museum?"

"No." A blush spread across her face.

"Did *you*?"

She gave her rich, sad laugh. "Well, jeez, Alton, there were all these mummies in the Egyptian section. I kept going around in circles, and I got tired, so I sat down for a second and took my shoes off."

In my mind, I saw Eloise sitting on the curb of Commercial Street, her shoes off.

Emily went on, playfully. "So I took a little nap, and when I woke up, I asked this guy where the exit was, and he showed me." She laughed. "He had to show me something else, too. He exposed himself to me next to the exit door."

"What did you do?"

"I waved goodbye."

I frowned.

"He was probably just trying to be friendly." Again, she laughed. "If it'd been Meg, she'd have said, 'Seen better.'"

Emily was looking at me in a teasing, measuring way. Behind her, the mountain had an icy pink tinge, and ground mist was coming up from the wet fields.

"Did you ever have a dog like Eloise did?" I was shivering.

"No." Her voice rose.

"Did you let him out in the halls like she did?"

"No."

"Did *you* carry a saddle around in New York?"

Bowing her head, she said sadly, "Eloise isn't me. I'm sorry."

As Emily turned from the dark, empty house, I all but expected her to disappear.

‡

That night as I stood guard in the Valiant, I went over the facts. There was the drawing of Eloise, or was she Meg? Eloise and my friend had both gotten lost in the Metropolitan Museum. I shook my head, thinking of the layers in the Michigan salt dome I'd done my thesis on— those old sea floors curled around themselves like layers of an onion. There were layers to Emily I hadn't seen.

I thought of how magma solidifies, some minerals cooling faster than others, forming dark blobs in the country rock, giving granite, for instance, a speckled, porphyritic texture. In fiction, there were these lumps of reality that got trapped. I didn't know which ones were fiction, which were real.

As I gripped the Valiant's steering wheel, the sky behind Emily's house and the notched fir trees of Sehome Hill was getting gray. I couldn't see the mountains. Another night's watch was done.

I started to turn on the engine when I heard motorcycles out front. Two men in helmets and black leather rode up Diamond Street, pulled over by the double spruce tree, and parked on Emily's lawn. I got out of the Valiant and crept alongside the house. I crouched in the shadows.

"Is she free? Is she easy? Is she caught?"

"She's easy. But she's caught."

"Who caught her?"

"Guy in Monroe."

"He's out?"

"He's out."

I ran out of the shadows. "Where's Eloise?" I cried.

The two men jumped up and kick-started their big engines. One man had a square face and stringy hair sticking out of his black helmet. I was pretty sure he was Merlin, AKA the Dink. He rode across Emily's lawn on his chopper, leaving ruts, then did a wheelie, and disappeared. The other man roared down the street, a gloved fist raised in the air.

Out of breath, I ran upstairs and pounded on Emily's door. In a minute, she answered sleepily, and I told her what I had seen.

"Alton, don't worry. The guy's locked up. I checked."

"But what about the Dink?"

She shook her head, frowning.

"Emily, we should call the cops."

"No."

"What about your P.I., Nevitt?"

"No."

Maybe he was fictional, too.

"At least let me stay on your couch tonight."

"That's not necessary." Her tone was edgy, accusing.

"But they were talking about Eloise. I know it."

"Dumb, dumb coincidences. I'm not letting them get to me."

I grasped Emily's elbow, but she pulled away, smiling sadly, clutching her bathrobe to her neck. "Now good night."

And she softly closed the door.

"Have it your own way," I called out to her closed door. Damn, she could be so unreasonable.

EIGHT

My watches the rest of the week were uneventful. Emily didn't again let me sleep on her couch, though we spoke on the phone most afternoons. She still hadn't found her missing jacket, and things kept breaking. "You haven't seen her, Alton?" she kept asking.

My stakeouts were like something in a story. I'd hunch in the shadows, waiting. A car would honk or a dog would bark. Wind blew through dark branches, and the moon went behind a cloud. Sometimes I got out of the Valiant, doing deep knee bends, feeling a heady sense of mission.

One night I dozed off and dreamt I was back in New York in a Puerto Rican neighborhood near 135th Street. Someone had opened a fire hydrant and flooded Riverside Drive. Traffic was stopped. Cars honked. It was hot. Kids splashed in a muddy lake in the street. The sewers were clogged. Turds and orange peels floated in the water, and a water buffalo lazed in the shallows under a Marlboro-man billboard. And there right in the smelly water sat Eloise, astride a white horse. She and the horse were covered with leeches, and she wasn't even trying to pull them off. She cried quietly, as if there were too much garbage or too many leeches or it was just too hot.

I came awake with a jolt. In my mind, I saw Eloise crying, and I held her. Or I lifted her from the white horse covered with leeches and cured her edema. Or I went with her to Enterprise Road. I'd be the hostage, instead of the Secretary of Agriculture. "I'll save you, Eloise," I muttered.

✝

My dog Landy was the only one I'd ever saved, and that was when I was eight.

Back in Riverdale, New York, Sundays had been our househunting days. My mother liked ranch houses and split-levels. My father liked neither, favoring our four-room apartment. I did, too. I had my room, my books of minerals, my window that looked out on the railroad bridge. "You can get along without your old man in the moon," my mother said. "You'll make friends."

One day my mother told Boomer the neighborhood was going downhill. The "element" was moving in. To her, that meant blacks and Puerto Ricans. I knew a lively discussion would soon get going.

My father said, "You want to drown us in some swamp in New Rochelle."

Thoughtfully, my parents included me in the discussion. From my mother, I heard such comments as "terrific chance," and "never forgive myself," while my father repeated his decision not to be drowned.

"Boomer, be reasonable. It won't cost anything to look. Then if you want to make us all miserable, you can."

An hour later, after a hunt for Landy who'd been hiding under the couch, we headed north on the Henry Hudson Parkway. The Olds ducked under the stone archways of overpasses, eating up the neat, black furrow in the middle of our lane. We cut away from the Hudson River and headed east on the Cross-Bronx Expressway.

We crossed a river, and my mother said, "New Rochelle."

"It's a swamp." My father scowled.

"Oh, shush," my mother said.

"Claire, watch the road. And stay under the speed limit. You're doing almost thirty."

"Oh, Boomer."

We turned onto a treeless drive where a billboard said *CHESHIRE ACRES*. When we parked by a brick ranch house with a muddy, unplanted yard, Landy's ears perked up. She always did like the country. My parents went inside, and Landy and I camped by a thin, brown stream running down the driveway. Where the stream met the sewer, we made a dam out of mud, sticks, and salt-and-pepper rocks that were probably granitic. A calico cat peeked out from under the Olds, showing a small, polite face framed by white paws. Landy gazed mournfully at her a few seconds, then took off, howling.

Soon her yelps turned plaintive. Her short legs, sunk in the mud, churned while she held her head up as if she were swimming or clambering through deep snow.

"Mommy! Daddy! Landy's sinking," I shouted.

My mother poked her head out the front door.

I pointed. "Do something. Please."

"Poor Landy," my mother murmured. "Boomer!" she called, and she kept saying "Poor Landy" over and over.

My father opened the door. "Don't anyone move. Not until we have a plan of action."

"But she's sinking," I said.

Landy rested her long jaw on top of the mud, wagging her tail softly, a look of resignation in her eyes. Her ears lay adrift in the mud like paddles.

"Alton," my mother said, "if I held on tight, do you think you could reach out and grab her?"

"And I'll hold onto you, Claire. Around the knees, so you don't slip," my father said.

"Poor Landy—"

"A center of gravity. A safety factor. Alton. Claire. Are we ready?"

"Mom, have you got me?"

"Claire, don't bend. You're tipping the center of—"

"I'm not tipping. Shush."

As my mother's fingers bracketed my ankles and my father supervised cheerfully, I stretched out in the mud, squirming on my belly toward Landy. The mud was warm and smelled nice the way it does when it melts on March afternoons. Landy picked up her head, and I stuck my hands down in the mud under her chin.

"Reach straight down, Alton," my father ordered. "You're reaching at an angle."

I settled for the hypoteneuse and hit one firm, churning paw and then the other.

"I've got her," I cried, grabbing hold.

"Good. When you're ready, say 'one-two-three,'" boomed my father.

"I'm ready now."

"Then say 'one-two-three.'" He was down on all fours, hugging my mother's knees. "Don't upset the safety factor."

"Oh, Boomer, one-two-three," said my mother disgustedly as she leaned back and pulled, and Landy shot out of the mud, simple as pie. The anchor man slipped forward on his face, and she sat down on top of him, her feet straddling his shoulders.

"Good work, Alton." My father gave me a beleaguered look from between my mother's knees. "But next time say 'one-two-three.'"

Landy shook herself, spattering us with mud. The calico cat waltzed up the driveway and batted at Landy's tail as she squirmed and trembled. I'd skinned my knee, and my ankles were traced with red welts.

"Alton, you saved her," my mother said, glowing.

"The safety factor saved her," said my father. "Claire, if that animal tracks any mud in the Olds, I'm dropping her at the Cross-Bronx Expressway."

"Oh, shush, Boomer," said my mother happily.

We piled in the Olds. We didn't buy the house. That day, one of the more reasonably wonderful ones of my childhood, had been almost like being in a story.

✝

On the day of her reading, Emily called me.

She sounded bright, edgy, sad. "I keep losing things. My mother gave me these earrings that were hers. And now—" She paused. "And my parents knocked this wall down in their house. They found Meg's old drawings, pictures of rivers and fields. They're so peaceful. But strange. We thought they were lost. Are you coming tonight, Alton?" she said in a rush.

That night Emily's students brought her a small feast— bean dips with guacamole, casseroles, pies, bread, pizza, chicken, juice, wine, beer. Six students read selections from their work. The small, wispy-bearded man who worked as a security guard read about a murderer who killed a woman after he saw his mother's features on the victim's face. In an offhand tone, Emily said she found the descriptions of the mother "touching in an awful way."

A young woman read a plotless story about planting tomatoes and red runner beans. A handsome, dark-haired man read a description of an oyster's point of view of a creative writing class, and he rang a bell to punctuate his sentences. Everyone praised him highly.

When Emily's turn came, she said she'd thought of writing *The Salvation Army Dress for Success Book*, a sequel to Eloise, though what she read wasn't about Eloise but about Meg. Emily read slowly, a pained, rapt look on her face:

> We spent the week at Newport. Meg and I slid down sand dunes and laughed about pineapple upside-down cakes. You see, their tops are on their bottoms. We laughed at Grandma who says "utterly" and likes gherkins, sour gherkins.

"I'm famished, utterly famished."

"Me, too. Have a gherkin."

When we left the beach, the sun was going down over the water. The sky over the dunes was pink, and we thought we saw the sun again. What was going on? It was the moon, a full moon. The sun hung above the water, and the moon regarded it silently.

When she was done reading, Emily looked up from her page at me, eyes wet. Then she went over to the dark-haired man, the expert on oysters. I wanted her to talk with me.

Later, she introduced me to her mother Sarah, a large, gray-haired woman whom I recognized from the photograph. She'd heard about me too, oddly.

As if welcoming me to the family, Sarah Weed chuckled and said warmly, "So you're the one who's fallen in love with the nutty Eloise?"

That was a fact, I admitted. "I've heard you found more of Meg's drawings."

She smiled. "It's almost as if she's coming back."

Emily, who perhaps had had too much to drink, swept me away and introduced me around as a writer who was living a novel—he just hadn't written it yet, she said. I protested I was a mere geologist who's taken a temporary leave of absence from his senses and fallen in love with Eloise. All of Emily's students gave me knowing looks. Raising my glass, I proposed a toast to Emily, whose writing I "esteemed and admired." I repeated my phrase several times.

Past midnight, we said our goodbyes out front by the double spruce tree. It was cloudy, mild, and the chinook wind blew out of the south. I'd lingered, the last one to go.

"Emily, it's meant so much," I began. Seeing her in her world, it was like being in her story.

"I'm glad," she said with a catch in her voice. She took my hand, leading me around back where we stood by her dead garden: three rows of withered cornstalks, four tall drooping sunflowers, some leafy things that had gone to seed, and behind them a sagging, unpainted picket fence and a few pumpkins, unharvested.

"This'll be the best year we've ever had," she said bravely, wistfully. Sighing, she glanced at her dead garden. "I should've put it to bed a long time ago."

"Did you get much out of it?" I asked.

"Tomatoes, corn, beans, zucchini—it was a wonderful garden," she said warmly.

"What's that?" I pointed to some purplish, leafy things.

"Cabbage. It bolted."

"And that?" I pointed to the fat leaves next to the pumpkins.

"Zucchini."

"You didn't turn them under?"

She squeezed my hand and turned to me, her eyes sad yet warm. "Alton, I didn't know I was going to make it through this year." She pronounced her words distinctly.

My stomach went tight.

"I didn't think I was going to see another spring or—" She paused, bowing her head. "I have a small confession to make. That doctor's appointment? It wasn't a check-up. I had to go in for some tests. It could've been cancer, but it wasn't." She bit the words off in her precise, unsentimental way.

My throat was hot and dry. All that time, she'd been sick, yet she'd listened to me about Eloise. I thought of when she cried in the Sirocco and when we chased her pages down her street.

"Ah, Emily," I murmured, looking down at my feet. "I've been so selfish."

"I'm going to live, Alton," she said fiercely. "Now all I've got to worry about is wrinkles and getting fat." She laughed with a strange gaiety.

"Did you tell your family?" I asked.

She shook her head, pursing her lips. The wind blew her dark hair up from her pale, thin face.

"I'm a dummy," I said. "I should've known."

"How could you know?"

So that was why she'd stopped writing.

"Alton, I've got another confession. I know your friend, Thelma. She introduced us. At folk dancing, last spring? You don't remember, do you?" She pronounced her words precisely.

Even Steven and Thelma were rarely seen in public together, but she and I had become friends. At the ferryboat folk dance last May, we'd danced a sprightly couple dance, "Road to the Isles"; a dreamy line dance, "Mana Vu"; then "Troika," a Russian dance. Spinning, twisting, cracking the whip, we swung a succession of third partners on as the boat churned over the bright water, Mount Baker blue-white in the distance, and the islands went up and down. I didn't remember meeting Emily.

"I'm sorry," I said.

She frowned. I hated her frown, but I wanted to hold her.

"You'll write again, Emily. I have faith in you."

"Stories don't change things."

"But they do!" Without the stories, I'd be at the bottom of Puget Sound, taking an extended leave of absence.

"I'm just so—" Grateful, I wanted to say, but that wasn't it, not all of it. I wanted her to write for herself, not me. "I'm sorry," I stammered.

Raising one hand, Emily made a sweeping gesture of largesse. And she smiled—elfin, prim, mischievous—a child still out playing after the streetlights had come on. Her green-brown eyes shining, she gazed up at me. I couldn't speak. Sighing, she glanced down at a rusty scythe that lay propped at her feet near the side of her white house.

"When you first wrote to me, Alton, I thought...." Her voice trailed off, a thrilling note of sadness, hope.

She glanced away, shuffling her feet, and stepped on something—the scythe. It bounced up and hit her head.

"Ouch, shit." She held her forehead, laughing, trying not to laugh. "These things keep happening, ever since...."

"Here, let me see." I leaned closer, and the handle of the scythe flew up and bopped me in the nose.

She laughed. "Oh, Alton, this is so crazy. It's happening to you, too, huh? Pretty soon...."

I shivered. Did she mean I'd be in her story?

Wiping her eyes, she bent toward me, rested one hand on my shoulder and gazed up at me.

In the light from the house, the cornstalks had a dead, bleached look like driftwood. The double spruce was tossing and heaving.

"I've stood guard out here all week," I offered.

"That's sweet, Alton."

"I'd feel better—you'd be more safe—if you let me sleep on your couch."

She smiled sadly. "No."

She turned, and we went around front. Eloise and I, we'd cut down the dusty stalks and turn them under.

As we stood by the front porch, Emily squeezed my hand, leaned up, and brushed my lips with her lips. She stepped back, bowing her head. In a firm, shy, slightly accusing way, she said, "Goodnight, Alton."

NINE

My phone rang as I trudged upstairs in the Bluestone. The rest of my watch had been uneventful. Banging through the glass doors, I stepped over Emily's pages on my faded carpet and picked up the phone. What if those yahoos on their choppers had come back?

A cooing voice murmured, "How are you, Alton?"

"Clarissa?" I asked, astonished.

"How are you?" she repeated, sighing.

I glanced out one corner of my window at the bay, which was made of smoke. A gray, drizzly dawn was breaking. My words came out too loud. "Are you with *him* now?"

"No, I'm not," she said, hotly. "I just—well, you never took anything. Not any of my jewels or even..." Her voice trailed off.

I thought her referral to three competent therapists had been more than enough. "What do you want, Clarissa?" I was dead-tired.

"I was hoping—" She sighed. "Hoping you'd want to work things through."

Shocked, I didn't answer.

Clarissa let out her breath, and her voice turned matter-of-fact. "Have you met your personnel committee yet?"

"No."

"Have you answered his letter?"

"No, and I'm not going to." I'd done my part, told him I needed a leave of absence. Blacking out before I could put my request in writing, that wasn't my fault.

"Oh, Alton," she said, "what about your career?"

"I don't have time for that now."

"Have you found your Eloise?"

It felt wrong hearing her say the name.

"Alton, I'm trying to help. I've always tried." She sounded practical, desperately practical. "You should see what he says, Alton," she offered, softly yet firmly. "He's not—"

"Not an unreasonable man? Goodnight, Clarissa." It was morning, but what the hell. I slammed down the phone. As I opened *Yes, I Don't Love You, Merlin,* Stevens' letter fell to the floor on top of Emily's pages.

I'll skim it and toss it, I thought. *Maybe Eloise will show up in a cloud of dusty sunlight. We'll tie handkerchiefs around our faces and join the demonstration in the head librarian's office. We'll toss tear gas canisters out the windows when the police come. We'll walk barefoot down Commercial Street, thumbing our noses. We'll lead campus security on chases in Brunhilda.*

I ripped open Stevens' envelope.

November 18, 1985

Dear Alton,

> *I'm aggrieved to inform you that, effective immediately, you are relieved of your duties at North Cascades University, formerly Cascadia College. Your note about going fishing indicates that you yourself wish for such a change.*
>
> *As you have not taught your classes since November 8, your contract demands that we take action as per this non-performance of your duties. If you had informed me in writing earlier, perhaps we*

might have arranged something for you. But the
matter is now, in point of fact, out of my hands.
   Your contract is terminated, effective November 15,
as per paragraph 45 in your contract, which states,
"This contract may be cancelled at the discretion of
the department chairman if he deems it in the interest
of the department."

Blah-blah-blah, he went on: appeals, thirty days, notify in writing. Resign, if you wish... Assist in finding you suitable... It ended, "I hope this year will be, in point of fact, a good one for you." He'd signed the letter, "Sincerely."

"Why'd he have to sign it like that?" I muttered, letting his page fall to the floor.

There was no dusty cloud of sunlight, no Eloise. My threadbare carpet stared up at me, as did my few remaining rocks on my bedroom bureau, my geode and my hunk of obsidian.

I had to get out.

‡

Rain was falling lightly as I walked down Holly Street, passing the park where I'd chatted with Mr. Nostalgia. Billows of smoke from the pulp mill spilled over the waterfront. I couldn't see the white houses of Sehome Hill across the bay. A dark freighter, the *Nix Beaman*, lay beached as a breakwater in front of a log boom. Gulls sailing over the steel tanks of Cascade Cold Storage uttered doll-like squeaks.

I went past the Light House Mission, the scrap metal yard, and the Salvation Army Thrift Store. I passed a row of waterfront bars—the Dirty Shame, the Salty Dog, the Eden Tavern. I smelled sawdust from the plywood factory and fish smell from the canneries. The wet air hung close, and I hugged my ski jacket around my neck.

On Railroad Avenue, across the street from Lerman's Pawnshop and the granite slabs of Nelm's Monuments, I paused in front of Dow Jewelers. Sixteen years ago, I'd bought Clarissa's and my wedding rings here.

The bright, impersonal-looking rings and watches gleamed in the display window. How sad Clarissa had sounded on the phone—sad and desperately practical—the way she'd sounded in the vault when she talked about her trysts with Stevens. She hadn't even sounded as if she enjoyed them. What she was really telling me, and telling herself, I thought, was that our marriage was over.

"Eloise, I'm not working anything through, ever," I said, digging my fingernails into my palms. As I faced the window, a picture of Clarissa and Stevens crossed my mind. Ten years ago on a winter night, we all had watched a Frankenstein movie on TV. Clarissa sat next to me on our couch. Across from us sat Stevens in an overstuffed red armchair we'd gotten at a garage sale. He'd helped us put our skylight in that fall.

Looking at him, Clarissa said, "Frankenstein can't ever die. He represents human qualities that can never die."

She's right, I thought. We never see Frankenstein die. He disappears in a torrent of water that topples a wall, or he stalks the battlements of a burning castle. We never see the bloated corpse or the singed body.

"I like to identify with monsters," said Stevens, raising his eyebrows slightly, grinning in a way that let us know he meant it. He glanced at me in his dry, friendly way. Then his eyes flicked back to Clarissa.

That night I dreamt I was Frankenstein, carrying a limp woman in my arms as I hunted for a way out of a burning castle. I staggered to the edge of a precipice, setting down the woman. I toppled over the edge. Then I stood chained in the burning castle, but the heat melted my chains and I burst free.

The next morning at breakfast when I told Clarissa my dream, she said, smiling, "You must like to identify with monsters, too."

"I don't identify with monsters," I said. "That's sadistic."

"Not necessarily," she said, smiling in a way that reminded me of Stevens' smile. "It's only a movie, Alton."

As her eyes met mine, I caught my breath. How was it that sometimes she seemed so close and other times she came from so far away? The islands were like that, distant on gray days, yet on clear days they stood out sharply.

I thought of how she'd smiled once when I asked her what she advised her clients about their sex lives.

"I tell them to enjoy themselves in whatever ways they like," she'd said, smiling.

"But what ways, Clarissa?"

She made a wry face.

"Poor monster," she said, smiling wistfully.

I thought that if she rubbed my neck, fur would grow on me. "If it isn't sadistic, it's masochistic," I said.

"I guess it is at that, Alton." She got up, coming around behind me, and she draped her arms around my neck.

☦

As I stared at the rings and watches at Dow's, I wondered who the monster was. Back then I thought Clarissa had meant me.

I'd asked Clarissa to marry me in December, three months after I met her in the hospital and she stared at me with her spirit eyes. My first summer in Sehome, I'd lived in the rooming house of two Croatian women who had emigrated to the Pacific Northwest because our coastline and mild climate reminded them of their country. One of the other tenants, a fisherman, also Croatian, used to say, "Once a woman set her sights on you, you a goner."

The day after Clarissa left the hospital, she asked if I'd come with her to family night, a group therapy session where each patient—or "member," as they were called— brought friends or family.

On a hot August night, we trudged down stone steps into the basement of a dimly-lit church, passing a gym where boys played basketball. Bells clanged upstairs, but down here it was cool. Clarissa introduced me, beaming in a shy, pleased way. An older woman tapped her cane angrily as she talked about how alone she felt when her daughter left to go to work. She went on in a hypnotic, muffled way for some time, until one of the counselors said her name, Melba, and paused. "I know you're scared," he said, "but can you try and live with it?"

As the woman wept, Clarissa held my hand and stared at Melba with a fixed look. Melba's daughter took her mother's hand, which still held the cane. After a second, Melba let go and the cane fell with a crack on the cement floor. Clarissa let out her breath; I squeezed her hand. A small man in a brown jacket and tie held up his withered arm with his one good hand and said, "We aren't allowed to love our counselors, and we can't love other members. Who can we love?"

Later, Clarissa took part in a group role-playing session called psychodrama. A long-faced man whose hair fell over his forehead enacted an imaginary confrontation scene with Clarissa playing the part of the man's wife who, he said, didn't love him. Sitting hunched on top of a long table, hugging his knees, the man said, "You never visited me in the hospital. You won't even come to family night."

Clarissa cut in and said, "You get me so mad talking about what I don't do. Why don't you do something for yourself?"

"What do you mean?" Boyishly, he hugged his knees to his chest.

Clarissa leaned forward. "Why don't you stand up?" she said coolly.

Shamefaced, he got up. His eyes had a forthright, stung look. He glanced around him like a rabbit. Then he yelled, "You bitch!"

Clarissa got up. One of the counselors, Jules, moved to step between them. But before he could, Clarissa raised her hand as if to slap the long-faced man. For a second, he stood there dazed, and then it sank in that he was about to be slapped, and he pulled his fist back in a slow, almost measured way.

Jules shouldered him out of the room. Clarissa murmured, "I shouldn't've done that." There was a silence.

That night we painted Clarissa's apartment yellow. Crying, she'd asked if I could ever love her after what she'd done. When I asked her to marry me, her eyes widened.

"Are you sure you want someone violent in your family?" she asked.

She didn't say yes that night, but on a bright December day, at the home of some friends on Lummi Island, Stevens gave the bride away. My parents flew out.

At the airport, my mother referred to Clarissa as "cat eyes," and raising one eyebrow, she said, "Boomer, it's because you made him use your shoetrees he's moved so far away."

"No, it's not," I said. I liked my father's shoetrees, or I used to.

"Then it's the way you made him shine your shoes," said my mother, frowning as if the insult had been to her.

"Claire, I never made him. And he moved out here for his job." My father rolled his dark eyes as if work, like marriage, were a bitter, obligatory grail.

In the house on Lummi Island, a picture window faced northwest. There weren't any islands, just open water, the Straits of Georgia, as far as we could see. When Clarissa and I said our vows, it was as if we were heading out into that clear, bright water.

‡

What stuck in my mind was Stevens and Clarissa at our wedding reception, both of them chuckling over a newspaper article I hadn't found funny. A man out walking his dog near St. Luke's Hospital had been shocked to see his pet retrieve a human foot that, it was later determined, had been amputated that day.

After the wedding, I called my parents less often. One time when my mother asked when they could come out and see me, Boomer said, "Cut the cord, Claire. Cut the cord." And the next spring, having told Clarissa about my parents' old passwords and barricades, I planted her birch tree on her birthday. In the spring, it put out such small, gold twigs.

On a warm April evening, Stevens, Clarissa, and I watched a TV show about reptiles. The smell of freshly-cut grass came from an open window. Clarissa was in therapy and had started school again. My classes were falling into place; my students weren't stealing my desk anymore. The one sad note was Stevens' then-wife Thelma, who often stayed home by herself and drank. Tonight she wasn't interested in any damn show about reptiles, he'd told us, shaking his head. In fact, she thought they were repulsive.

"Oh, they are," Stevens admitted, meeting my eyes. Seated in our old red armchair, he smiled drily yet warmly, as if pleased to own up to the small flaws of his good friends, proud he could see them in perspective.

"That iguana," said Clarissa, turning to Stevens, "the one with the armor around its neck? That's you." She smiled brightly, yet mockingly.

"And that's *you*," he said, not missing a beat. The TV screen showed a frilled lizard with its mouth—or rather, its beak—opened wide as if to shriek. The frilled lizard clacked its beak closed, then opened it, expanding a kind of hood or headdress around its neck.

"And just like it, I'm not at all dangerous," she said.

The lizard was poised to strike.

"You both take these animal shows very seriously," I said. I'd started to say "very personally," but that seemed risky, not clearly a fact.

"How can you *not* take them seriously?" asked Clarissa, laughing. "Look at them, Alton. Now that's us."

Two giant Galapagos turtles were trying to mate. The male—I assumed it was the male—crawled onto the back of the female, straddling her, his flippers splaying the air, his thin neck poking down towards her head, which kept darting and jerking like a bird's neck or a snake's.

"The poor things," Clarissa said, squeezing my arm. "Look at him trying to find her under all that tortoise shell. Why, they look like two armored cars trying to do it."

"Clarissa, don't make fun of them." I pointed out that the announcer had called reptiles the first creatures to fertilize the egg within the female, so, of course, their first attempts would be crude.

"He's right." Stevens was laughing.

Clarissa started laughing, too. A giggling attack swept the two of them, and I tried to laugh along, but I was having a hard time, for I didn't see what was so funny.

"Cut it out, you two," I said, frowning. "I can't hear what he's saying." I stared at the screen, trying to concentrate.

Clarissa and Stevens laughed harder. As I tried to ignore them, the decibel-level of their hysterics went up. Clarissa covered her eyes and gasped; Stevens' laugh had a dry, cackling sound I didn't think was worthy of him.

I'd always been interested in reptiles. As a child, I had dreams about dinosaurs, and during the day at school, if things got boring, I pictured my make-believe friends. Snow, Tongue, and Wednesday would fight along with the stone men and women who saved the good dinosaurs (plodding Brontosaurus and dim-witted, razor-backed Stegosaurus) from the predator Tyrannosaurus Rex.

The TV show had moved on to crocodiles in Egypt. The announcer said the female buries her eggs in the mud of the Nile. After a few months, when the eggs are ready to hatch, she goes back and digs them up, closing her teeth around them and delicately swimming them upstream.

One by one, she deposits her eggs in a new site on the riverbank that she and the bull crocodile take turns guarding. When the young crocs pop out of the eggs, a few slither into their parents' mouths, hiding in those grinning, gap-toothed cages.

As a child, I used to wake up at night after a scary dream about dinosaurs. My father would come into my room and sit on my bed, explaining that the dinosaurs died out millions of years ago.

"They're extinct, Alton." His teeth were shining in the dark.

"I know they're all stinked," I said. "The book said so." But if they were dead, how could I be dreaming of them?

I started crying, and my father told me not to worry, and I tried to stop crying so he wouldn't feel bad, but that just made me cry harder.

Now the TV screen showed crocodiles basking in the sun, opening their mouths wide. The harder Clarissa and Stevens tried to stop laughing, the harder they laughed. I told myself not to be paranoid. It probably wasn't me they found so funny. It was unreasonable to expect myself to get every joke people laughed at for whatever weird reason, and I waited for them to stop.

The crocodiles gaped their jaws wide, cooling the roofs of their mouths. Stevens' chortles had turned to weak, dry wheezes; tears ran down Clarissa's cheeks.

I shut my eyes, going over hypotheses that explain the Cretaceous extinction of the species. A commercial came on. Clarissa and Stevens had stopped laughing.

"What a great show," I said.

✢

As the rain fell harder, the rings in Dow's display window gleamed, and I took off my ring. I *would* pawn the damn thing.

An odd picture crossed my mind. Stevens and my wife kissed as a heap of black-and-yellow snakes coiled around their legs. Behind them, two crocodiles lumbered out of a flat, brown river, their almost legless bodies crackling in the underbrush. Then the two animals were grinding their bodies together, coupling, both of their mouths gaped wide. Stevens and Clarissa laughed and laughed, gasping.

I let out a cry. Under the fluorescent lights, the edges of the bright rings wavered. I knew I hadn't seen real crocodiles, but the picture had been so clear, like one in a dream. For a second I was back in the vault, feeling for the edge of Clarissa's deposit box. Did I really want a weapon? I could get a gun in Lerman's Pawnshop.

The picture of the crocodiles came over me, and I doubled over, sick to my stomach. I went to the curb and leaned out into the street like a poor, dumb turtle, wanting to throw up or get my head lopped off. I didn't care which. My chest ached, my diaphragm squeezing its way out of my rib cage. *I could kill them both. Shoot them like a coil of snakes. We're all animals.*

The crocodiles' mouths were clamped together....

I threw up then. I was crying, too.

As I turned and pulled myself up, something—a shadow—flickered across the bright display window.

"Eloise," I cried out.

Shuddering, I stared through my own reflection at the rows of earrings, rings, and bracelets glinting arrogantly behind the glass. It was time I had a word with my friend Stevens.

TEN

B ack in the Bluestone, I slugged down three cups of
coffee, dragged a razor across my face, and called it
a new day. I drove south down Chuckanut Drive. In the
rain, the gray water looked brighter than the sky. Letting
the Valiant stutter past the stone lions by the entrance
to Fairhaven Park, I shifted gears, lunged downhill past
the glum rows of trailer homes, then climbed into a rift
in a hill of fir trees that closed darkly behind me. The
wet trees looked bedraggled. Soon the woods opened,
and I pulled into a down-sweeping driveway just short
of the scenic overlook.

The house was Thelma's now. I was used to dropping in
unannounced, ever since she and Stevens separated and I
became godfather to their daughter Constance. I needed
to know more about Stevens' liaisons with my wife. I
needed an ally.

The house jutted over the bay on stanchions. Triangular
glass panels gleamed like obsidian, dark cedar shakes
blending into the hillside. I knocked at a big round-
shouldered door and, when no one answered, let myself
in. I stood in the hallway, whistling "Green Onions,"
Eloise's wake-up song.

"Hi, Alton," said Thelma in a strained, cheerful voice, as she came down the stairs, coffee cup in hand.

I moved my lips, but nothing came out. I went across her gold living-room carpet and sat down in the big fireplace.

"Why don't you light a fire and cook me?" I said loudly. "Just about everything else that could've happened has happened."

Thelma smiled in her deceptively childlike way. A year younger than me, she'd always seemed older. She had pale skin, straight blond hair, and thin features, attractive in a way.

"You know about me and Clarissa?" I asked, wiping soot from my lips.

Thelma nodded and asked kindly, "How are you, Alton?"

I craned my neck. "And Stevens, you knew about him?"

She nodded and smiled again. "Answering a question with a question, Alton—are you sure you aren't Jewish?"

When I didn't answer, Thelma, who was Jewish, said, "There's a saying: a Jew answers a question with a question."

"I'm becoming a saying," I muttered. "How about an eye for an eye, eat or be eaten? How long have you known, Thelma?"

She shrugged. There was a vague, old-world quality about Thelma that showed at odd moments. "About my husband, oh, I've always known. I didn't want to believe it, but I knew. About Clarissa? Not so long ago."

The prattling way she raised questions and ticked them off made me feel I was being kept after school. Her throaty undertone reminded me of Clarissa's mother, an elegant woman with a Slavic face and watery eyes. I'd met her just once.

"He isn't what he made us think, is he?" I asked.

"Whatever we thought, we thought." Her voice had a shrugging sound, as if she weren't so much resigned as matter-of-fact, ready for what came next.

"He had affairs before we married, and he had them after," she continued in her singsong way.

Dim light sifted down the dark cedar walls and pooled around the clean yellow beams that held up the vaulted ceiling. When I picked myself up, Thelma gave me a melancholy smile, as if she found something sad in the way I braced myself.

I remembered the first time I'd met her in this house, sixteen years ago. It had been my first evening in the Northwest, and Stevens had brought me here to meet members of the North Cascades family. Thelma's pale face had a stern look. She told me she liked to spend her days window-shopping at the old Sehome Mall. On one hand, her fingernails were bitten down, and she kept them short, she told me, so that she could finger a guitar keyboard.

On his baby grand piano, Stevens played the "Moonlight Sonata" like a decorous lullabye. He peered down his nose at the sheet music as if he were snubbing it. Dr. Doll, a bearded man with intense dark eyes, said the world's biggest supply of dunite sits in the Twin Sisters, two saw-toothed peaks south of Mount Baker. Dr. Sandman, whose specialty was metamorphic rock, told me sedimentary rocks are low class. I frowned; that was my specialty.

It was hot, so I pulled my sweater over my head. For a second, my arms were caught. Then they weren't. And there was Thelma, smiling sadly, as if trying to tell me something. She seemed sad for me, as if she knew something was going to happen to me, and I wondered if that same thing had happened to her.

Now as I stood by Thelma's fireplace and she smiled her sad smile, it seemed that same thing *had* happened, and I'd found my way here by dead reckoning. Maybe the place I'd made my start in this far corner of the country would get me going a second time.

"You know I've been fired?"

She nodded. "You're going to accept it?"

Facts were facts. The receptionist had seen me having my imaginary conversation in the Counseling Center. And I had put that *GONE FISHING* sign on my office door.

"You can appeal, can't you?" asked Thelma kindly. "And he has made enemies. Former students—former lovers, I should say—they might have something to tell you. He keeps all these old files, too. Every letter he ever sent or got, God knows what." She bit the words off with a forlorn flair.

"Why haven't you talked to those women yourself?"

Shrugging, she laughed in a throaty way. "And what makes you think I haven't?"

"It shouldn't have happened to either one of us," I said.

She shook her head and said, smiling, "But Alton, I have all I need."

I thought she was going to survey her gold carpet, her fieldstone fireplace, the bay outside her window. But three-year-old Constance bounced into the room, chasing their gray cat, Tinker.

"Alton eating breakfast?" asked Constance, giving me a hug. We liked to tell each other stories.

"No, honey, Alton can't stay," said Thelma.

I glanced at my watch, almost eight o'clock, when a rattling in the chimney startled me. There in the empty fireplace lay a bird's nest like a dessicated crown.

Constance broke into tears, ran up, and hugged my knees. "Alton, put it back. They'll *need* it."

"No, honey." I bent to hug her. "They had to move."

I got up and turned toward the door. As I glanced back over my shoulder, curling my fingers, waving a little, the smile on my face felt frozen.

☦

Stevens' new place was northeast of town on Grunion Road. As I passed the stone lions guarding the chopped-back arms of the rose bushes in Fairhaven, a hot, dry wind was blowing through my bones.

On Railroad Avenue, I pulled over by the pawnshop and got rid of my wedding ring for a hundred bucks. I didn't look at the racks of rifles on the walls. I got back in the Valiant, headed out the Mount Baker Highway, and crossed the swollen Nooksack River. On a gravel road, I turned off and went uphill past a line of alders and a stubble field. On a bare knoll under the dark hills stood Stevens' house.

Two gateposts flanked his driveway, each one tapering into the sculpted faces of two women. Built from clay rings, they used to remind me of fossilized coral reefs. Now the women jutted up like tokens of tribute. Painfully, scornfully, the women gazed out as if their struggle to become something different from the clay they came from had distorted them and made them grotesque.

Once Stevens told me how when he and Thelma made love, he liked to think he was hurting her, and one time she'd told him, "It hurts good." Now I wondered what Clarissa went through in her so-to-speak, off-and-on relationship with him. So he raised me from a pup, did he?

I banged the brass knocker on his big, black door that loomed like a drawbridge. I wasn't used to dropping in here. The door creaked open, and a thin section of Stevens' face winced at me.

"Remember me?" I asked brightly, as if nothing had happened. "Can I come in?"

"I don't see why you'd want to." He opened the door about one-sixth more, gazing past me like the women on his gateposts. I told myself what had happened had really happened. Oddly, the thought made me feel relieved.

"Is Clarissa here?" I demanded.

"No, in point of fact. You didn't—you don't want to—surely—"

"It's you I want to talk to." I pushed past him.

He stepped back briskly and made a sardonic, waving gesture, closing his small mouth like a mail slot.

"If it's about my letter," he said rapidly, "I don't want to hear it. You can reply in an official capacity."

Behind him in the big dim hallway hung a drawing of a nude man. I lowered my eyes. For a second, I couldn't seem to remember what I'd come here for or what I wanted to say.

"There is something you might look at, while you're here, Alton." He turned and walked away from me in his alert, wiry way.

I thought of another time he walked away. It was during the spring when we watched the show about reptiles. I'd dropped by when he and Thelma were in the middle of a fight. He'd held his head up stoically as Thelma screamed curses from upstairs, and he said in his resigned way he'd better go up. Pursing his lips, he savored the situation like a wine maker testing his newest wine's rare, acrid bouquet—for better or for worse, for richer or poorer, in sickness and in health.

Now as he padded away and glided upstairs, I could've sworn he was going to tell Thelma I'd come to visit. He seemed that unconcerned.

I went into the living room and stood by his fireplace, trying to think of what to say. "You weren't my friend," I muttered. But that didn't sound right. I kicked one of the black leather sofas that studded his white carpet. Beside his fireplace, a pair of black tongs sat propped up like two small spears. Upstairs, what sounded like metal file drawers banged open, closed.

His living room was heraldic. A long, black, glass-topped coffee table holding his eighteenth-century set of mole-headed ivory chess pieces, part of his inheritance, shone like a family crest. Across from it stood his slab of chocolate-brown, Precambrian shield rock cut across by younger pegmatite dikes. The shield rock was nearly four billion years old. On a tall black counter sat his cases of numbered, labeled fossil specimens, just back from loan to a museum of paleontology in Boston.

The needles of the *Metasequoia occidentalis*, similar to Dawn Redwood, were living fossils, the label said. I'd always liked the way the needles that had fallen softly to the earth forty million years ago seemed etched into the Chuckanut sandstone by an artist's hand. I admired the *Equistium newberrye*, relative of the common horsetail that can be found growing beside railroad tracks. Stevens had set a modern horsetail next to the fossil, and the striations at the joints matched.

Stevens' favorite was number twenty-seven, *Sobalitis ingeri*, whose long leaf tapered like a black-and-gray fan big as your hand. He'd collected it, he said, on the Chuckanut Formation. "All the big boys said the faulting was shallow. But in point of fact," he'd told me, grinning, "no one ever looked. That same day I found the *Sobalitis*, in an outcrop in a stream bed that showed the faulting wasn't shallow. Two in one day."

I'll prize out the Dawn Redwood or the Sobalitis, I thought. But I didn't know which one to take—his favorite or mine. His shield rock eyed me as if it knew things. On one wall hung a Kwakiutl Indian mask Clarissa had fondly named the Dying Warrior. His heavy-lidded and pain-filled eyes drooped above a strong jaw with a swollen mouth distended in a grimace. The Warrior's thick lips and big canines couldn't hold in his bulbous tongue. He was choking.

I turned, and Stevens was there, holding an envelope. He glanced at the Warrior and, referring to a Kwakiutl legend he'd once told me about a spirit that took young men into the forest and taught them to eat human flesh, he murmured, "Hungry, Alton?" There was a flicker of amusement in his voice. He handed me the envelope.

I'll eat him alive, point-of-fact him. "What I am is mad," I said, but I opened the letter.

"Clarissa said you wanted the truth." He shrugged, raising one eyebrow. "It's time to leave the nest, Alton." He gave me a Cretaceous little smile.

The letter was from Clarissa, addressed to him. For a second, I thought maybe she'd come to her senses. Maybe she'd moved in with him for a few days and found he wasn't as reasonable as he seemed.

I read:

> *We'll still see each other, won't we? Who cares how often? Only kids count. It's being here that matters, biting into what we need to live. All the years weren't wasted because they brought me to this turning point, this jumping off point, I should say. You've been a better friend than you bargained on. It was a long, hot summer. I won't pretend I know what comes next, but I know I'm ready for it, come what may. Goodbye.*
>
> *Love, Clarissa.*

"Not exactly a love letter, is it?" asked Stevens drily.

"I wouldn't know. I'm a man of facts." I glanced at the postmark, July 13, 1969. That had been the summer I met her. What did she mean, "all the years"? She'd made her suicide attempt when her first marriage ended.

"You knew her back then?" I cried.

Part of me told myself in a point-of-fact voice that if he'd known her first it was reasonable that he got first crack at her, so to speak. My chest felt tight, and I hoped I wouldn't have to throw up again. This seemed like neither the time nor the place.

Stevens leaned against his shield rock languidly, gazing at me with a dusty look.

"You *knew* her?" I repeated.

He shrugged, budged his frown lines up, and said, "You never really liked me, Alton. You wanted someone to tell you what to do. I did step on your toes a bit, but that was mostly before—" He broke off, pursing his lips with distaste. "Look at it this way. If it weren't for me, you'd never have gotten to know her. Who told you to call up that woman with the sex survey?"

"But you were like a father to me."

"Well, now I'm sending you into the world where there aren't any heroes or saints, but just people trying to... make things happen."

He held his palms up in an oddly plaintive way, then stroked his chin, as if like the clay women guarding his driveway he had nothing more to say.

"Why?" I shouted.

"Alton, I'm not going to get down on the floor and grovel for you. Both of you should thank me, and neither one of you is grateful."

"Grateful?"

"Yes, I was your buffer zone, your neutral territory, your DMZ At least Clarissa wanted to know how things work. You...." He held his palms up, empty.

"You're not sorry, are you?"

"No, I'm not."

"You *will* be."

"In point of fact, this conversation's getting repetitious."

I'll crush the Dawn Redwood down to coal, to a diamond, and cut things with it. I shoved Clarissa's letter into my pocket.

"Just a minute." Stevens moved closer. "My papers don't leave the premises."

"Your papers? She's my wife."

"And she was mine, too, Alton. Before she knew you."

"Yours?" I repeated, numbly.

"Not my wife, but *mine*." Stevens' small eyes bulged out. "She was mine when I helped you win her, mine when I helped you keep her. She's mine even now when she—"

"Shut up!" I yelled.

It was weird, but his face turned wistful.

The picture of the crocodiles merged with him and my wife.... I bent over, gasping. *I'll take something or break something, put gravel in the gas tank of his 1933 Chrysler Silver-Wraith. Hack the clay women down from their gateposts, bury them in the fallow field across the road. Steal the Silver-Wraith, spray-paint "Fucker" on the windows.*

"Eloise!" I called out.

And I heard her, talking from what seemed like the inside of my head. "Alton, go tell him he's a prick."

"Eloise—where? How?"

"Just tell him, Alton. I can't keep this up for long."

Stevens was backing away from me, eyes wide.

"You prick," I said lamely. I said it again, "Prick, prick," and felt better. "You're a prick, you fucking prick!" I went over to the fireplace and picked up the poker.

"Alton, don't do anything you'll be sorry for." It was Eloise, her voice fainter, coming from the Dying Warrior.

Tightening my grip on the poker, I went over to the Warrior and lifted him off his hook on the wall.

"Put that down, Alton," said Stevens quietly. "Have you lost your senses?"

"I have." I raised the poker.

Stevens grabbed my arms and spun me around. I pulled away, dropping the Warrior, and we fell to the floor. Stevens kicked and bit like a small, bony animal. We wrestled the poker back and forth. With a jerk, I wrenched the thing out of his hands. His neck snapped back, and his head hit the tile fireplace with a thud.

Eyes closed, he lay there. Beside him, the Warrior eyed me dolefully.

"You'll be here now when I need you, won't you, Eloise?"

Kneeling down, I picked up the Warrior, then got up and staggered toward the door. As I went past the mole-headed chess pieces, they smirked at me. I turned around.

Stevens lay curled up by his shield rock, small and crumpled.

What if I'd killed him? Shaking, I went over, knelt down, and pressed my hand against his wrinkled neck. I felt no pulse. I pressed harder. He groaned, and I jumped back. His closed eyes knew things I'd never know.

Cradling the Warrior, I got up and ran to the door, heaved it open. There was my Valiant, looking as if it had caught me in the act.

ELEVEN

Panting, I stood in the driveway. Beyond Stevens' gateposts and the stubble field, the dark hills stretched out to the Twin Sisters' sharp peaks with their secret hoard of dunite. "He's a prick," I muttered.

The foothills' right angle to the mountains was caused by transform faulting, or so he'd said. I didn't know. I wasn't up on these suspect terrains, backed into the continent, crunched and practically cremated.

"Eloise," I murmured, turning toward Stevens' garage door, which yawned half open. Deep in the shadows lurked his Silver-Wraith, its whitewalls fluffy as pillows, its round black fenders gleaming like enormous knees. By the right front tire sat a can of spray paint.

I went over and heaved the door open, picked up the paint can. *Eloise, we'll paint our faces black, ride like John Brown's men to Harper's Ferry. Join the Vegetarian League.* Slowly, as if detonating a bridge or a cathedral for the good of the free world, I opened the nozzle.

Black paint streamed out. I made a drippy capital *P*, then broke into a rough script, covering the front and rear windows with the logo, *Prick*. But I didn't want to be seen driving *that*. The paint would block my vision, too. I let the paint can fall.

"Hop in, Alton," called Eloise in her scratchy voice from somewhere out in the light.

I picked up the Warrior and peered outside. She was sitting behind the wheel of my Valiant. Smiling, squinting, she turned the ignition and honked the horn. The silver scrolls on her oriental jacket were faded. Her wide-set eyes, almost all pupil, were a honey-gold like nothing in the world except maybe the eyes of large cats.

Gripping the steering wheel with both hands, she gunned the engine. I ran to her.

"I have to look at you," I said, leaning my head in the window.

"That's sweet, Alton. Jump in. That creep's gonna call the cops."

She grinned, revving the engine, and something in me pulled sideways.

"Alton." Frowning, she pointed, and I turned. Stevens' thin face peeked from behind the curtains.

I got in, and she rammed my car backwards. "Hooowheee!" she shouted in a cloud of gravel.

"Hoo-whee," I said, getting in the spirit of things.

Tires screeching, we pulled onto the road heading toward town. But there was one small problem. We weren't heading, we were barreling backwards on the Mount Baker Highway. Eloise hadn't thrown the Valiant into forward gear.

The gateposts got smaller, and the stubble field flew away. Only the dark hills kept up with us. Eloise had one arm on the seat-rest, her head swung around as she peered back, her short brown hair blowing across her forehead.

The Valiant moaned, up near fifty. My stomach felt tight. "Eloise, uh, wouldn't it be more reasonable—"

"Relax, Alton. I've got it under control." She shot me a deadpan look, then grinned.

Emily wasn't writing this, or I didn't think so. I swallowed hard.

"This is super," said Eloise, her gold eyes glowing. "Ever since I lost Brunhilda...."

She broke off, a frank abashed look on her face and such dancing, yellow flecks in her eyes. A dull shock went through my solar plexus. *Oh God, is she looking at me with amusement or wonder?*

Eloise flexed the fingers of one hand, touched her face, her neck. Stretching, she leaned back, bracing herself against the steering wheel. She rotated her shoulders, one at a time, as if they were stiff.

If Emily could see us now, I thought, and the Valiant swerved onto the shoulder, kicking up dust.

"Uh, Eloise, would you please—"

"No problem, Alton." She swung the wheel, and we went up on two wheels, doing sixty, and then we were down. My real life streamed away like so much debris. I didn't know what came next or what we were leaving behind.

She glanced over with her calm, impersonal interest, her eyes glassy and dilated. *Maybe she's been smoking something? Oh, Emily.*

Again, the Valiant teetered on two wheels. The Twin Sisters reeled sideways, then straightened up.

"Uh, Eloise," I said, pressing my abdomen, "let's head to town."

"Your place, Alton?" She gave me a sideways grin. "Now we're cooking."

"We should go see Emily," I said.

"What for?" Eloise punched the Valiant up past seventy, swinging around a logging truck as we went uphill.

Yes, now and forever, what for? The wind blew her hair across her forehead as she leaned her compact body into the curve. Considering this was her first time behind the wheel of a real car, she was doing pretty well.

A car came at us over the top of the hill, its driver an old woman, eyes wide with fear. Eloise swung the wheel, slammed on the brakes, and we veered, shimmying, in front of the logging truck whose red-faced driver shook his fist.

When I turned to Eloise, she was gone. "Oh, shit!" I grabbed the wheel, pulling hard as I tromped on the brake and promptly sailed into a spin.

I recited the ages—Triassic, Jurassic—when dinosaurs lumbered slowly, oh, so slowly. The fields and foothills swung around. The dinosaurs rolled over dead in the Cretaceous extinction of the species. The Valiant came to rest on the side of the road, having made a 360-degree spin. The engine died. The logging truck blew by with a blast on its air horn.

I turned the ignition and it caught. Taking big gulps of air, I eased up through the gears until I was doing a more reasonable forty-five miles per hour.

I headed back to Sehome, crossing the narrow iron bridge over the Nooksack River, its sandbars and glacial till half-hidden, mist drifting over the dark foothills. Back in town I took the freeway, got off near the hospital, and turned onto Diamond Street. I rammed the Valiant onto Emily's sidewalk, then ran upstairs. When I knocked, the door came open. I reached for the handle, and it clattered to the floor. Scratches, fresh pry marks, showed on the wood of the doorframe.

"Emily!" I called out and ran inside.

No answer. Her typewriter and box of crayons sat on her desk, and her hanging plants draped down. I went into the kitchen. The drawing of the three women was gone.

Outside, a motorcycle roared. I went to the window. A man with long hair streaming out of his black helmet raced down the alley on a big motorcycle. It was Merlin, AKA the Dink. I ran downstairs, but he was gone.

Trembling, I drove to a phone booth near the Miracle. I dialed the university, got the English Department. A blustery someone told me Ms. Weed had called in sick.

"She's not sick," I said.

I slammed down the phone, called the police to report a

break-in on Diamond Street. When the dispatcher asked my name, I dropped the phone. I stood there, gasping. In a minute, I called Thelma. No answer.

I conferred with the Warrior. Emily was in trouble. And if I found her, she'd probably want to arrest me for stealing her pages. I was a thief, a monster. If I went back to the Bluestone, the cops would probably be waiting. The Warrior grinned.

My father says the reasonable thing to do when you're looking is to wait. *I should call him. It's been more than a month.* The last time we'd talked, I'd told him I didn't need any more shoetrees for my birthday this year.

"You don't?" he'd boomed, sounding injured.

The sky will crack open and a ram's horn will blow if I tell him I wear Hush Puppies and don't use shoetrees.

"Eloise, I'm heading back to the Bluestone," I muttered. If the cops were waiting, so be it.

As I staggered up my front steps, my landlady Miss Bosom was planting something in a window box that resembled another Swedish Ivy. I raised the Warrior in salute. She grinned her big-cheeked grin. Upstairs, I sat and waited. Anchored by my geodes, Emily's pages lay there like a ransom. Eloise would have to find me where I said I'd be.

I put on the Warrior mask and took out Clarissa's letter. In this remnant from my B.C. life, Clarissa thanked my mentor in an ardent, desperate tone, saying he'd been a friend to her since her first husband Tor died. She went on in a hypnotic way—unable, it seemed, to stop—chanting, almost praying. "I kept trying to go with him, to die, to go back. You were my savior, my—"

I was crying. Clarissa had never told me about other suicide attempts. I took off the Warrior, setting him down on top of a pile of Emily's pages. The hot, dry wind was in my throat. My wrists were freezing.

Shaking, I dug out Clarissa's new number I'd scribbled down when she called. I dialed, and a man answered.

"Where's Clarissa?" I shouted.

"Who the hell are you?"

"Her husband. Excuse me, who are you?"

"A friend." His voice was mild, soft, deep. "She said if you called, to tell you she's gone Back In."

The hospital.

"I'm not calling her, Eloise—I'm not," I said, putting down the phone, and I ran and got *Yes, I Don't Love You*. I read out loud: "Eloise Hartwig stared at the wreck of her VW Bug, Brunhilda."

Damn, I had to find her before the League kidnapped the Secretary.

✧

Slowly, my door opened, and she stood there, the big E, head down, one hand over her eyes. Her shoulders slumped as she leaned heavily against the doorframe.

I ran to her. "Eloise, what happened?"

I put my arms around her, but she shrugged me off.

"Dammit, she's making me do things," she muttered angrily, shaking her head.

"Who? You mean Emily?"

She nodded, seeming to scrunch herself inward, as if she were in a painful struggle.

"How can she do that?" I asked, amazed yet wanting the facts.

"I can't be in two places at once, Alton," she said, narrowing her red-rimmed eyes. She'd been crying.

I didn't like to hear her downgrade herself. If anyone could be in two places at once, Eloise could.

"Why'd you take off like that?" I asked.

"I had to. I can't stay here."

She didn't sound sure of where "here" was.

"But where'd you go, Eloise?"

She shook her head. "Just hold me, Alton."

She leaned against me, and I held her. I didn't move. Soon she started talking in a slurred, halting way.

"They've got—" She paused, looking around her.

"The Secretary of Agriculture?"

"Yes. In the house—"

"On Enterprise Road?"

"And the Dink—"

"You mean Merlin?"

She nodded, then looked at me wildly. Her voice rose into a scratchy wail. "Shit, shit, she said we were through. She promised."

Her lips pulled up on one side in a sad smile, a bit like Emily's.

"But that can't be," I said reasonably. "She hasn't written in six months."

"Believe me, she's making me do things."

I glanced down at Emily's first drafts on my floor.

"Where else did you go, Eloise?"

"There was... a battlefield. I was taking pictures... rolls of film. Something about a newspaper, *Passages*, and talking to soldiers, taking notes. Then I was a child... near a lake, telling stories. She writes them down and gets all the credit. It's not fair."

Angrily, Eloise said, "Alton, I'm not gonna be one of those split—whatchamacallem—schizomatics?" She stepped out of my arms and stood squarely, arms crossed, squinting out of her gold eyes.

She kicked one of my geodes off of a pile of Emily's pages. "Ouch. Shit, shit!" she shouted, hopping on one foot. "I hate her. I'm not doing a damn thing for her."

It hurt me to hear her speak of Emily with such bitterness.

"There's something else, Alton," she said, regarding me with curiosity, more than curiosity, her eyes glowing. I gave her my Rock of Ages grin. Maybe my steadying influence would help her stick around.

"When my book lady—" She paused.

"Hijacks you?"

She nodded. "I'm with you. In a vault."

I shivered. "In cubicle number three?"

"Uhn uh." She shook her head.

"In number one?"

She frowned; I frowned.

"In number two?" I'd never been in number two.

She tried not to smile. "It gets pretty hot in there, Alton."
Then in a sad, abashed way, she asked, "You can't forgive
her yet, can you?"

I hung my head.

"Don't be bitter, Alton."

Me, I was the elephant who couldn't forget. She should
know that. She knew so much else.

Eloise sat down on my faded carpet beside a pile of
Emily's pages. She clenched and unclenched one hand
painfully, then rested both hands in her lap. On one wrist
she wore a plastic hospital I.D. bracelet.

"Where'd this damn thing come from?" she asked.

I shrugged.

Eloise frowned, her eyes flat and empty. She got up,
ripped off the plastic bracelet, and threw it on the floor.

"She's not putting me in the hospital, Alton. Just because
she's sick."

I didn't get it. In the stories, Eloise had worn a bracelet
of dental floss taped around her wrist, not this thing. Sure,
I'd compared it to Clarissa's hospital bracelet once. "Back
In," the man had said. For a second, I pictured myself
walking down a hallway toward the solarium, Clarissa
asking, "Are you my doctor? Are you my father?"

Telling myself to be reasonable, I ran and got *Yes, I Don't
Love You.* When I turned to the part where Eloise flosses
thirty minutes a day, I read it aloud, but Eloise laughed
scornfully. "No one flosses that much. I don't."

"But you did, Eloise," I said admiringly, showing her
the book.

She moved her lips, frowning, then pushed it away in disgust. Glancing down at Emily's pages on my floor, she asked in a matter-of-fact way, "Are you writing my novel, Alton?"

"No." I was blushing.

"Well, what's all this?" Eloise nudged my geode off its pile of pages, picking up the chapter where she had been vacuuming in the occupied building as the Youngbloods blared on the stereo.

"I rescued them, sort of." I told her about the night Emily threw out her first drafts.

"Now she's gone, Eloise, and her place was broken into. And I saw the Dink. I think Emily's in trouble."

Eloise pursed her lips, unimpressed.

"We've got to go see...." I paused. "Your creator."

"She's not my creator."

"Do you know where she is?"

"No, Alton." Eloise squinted at me. "You sure *you're* not writing my novel?"

I glanced down at the pages. "I'm just the custodian."

"And you *stole* these pages?" She sounded impressed.

I nodded, wondering if stolen goods had added value for Eloise. No, that was unworthy.

"Could the Dink have followed you here?" I asked.

"Maybe. I don't know." Touching my hand, she gazed up frankly, hopefully, with what seemed like more than love, an impersonal love, understanding or forgiveness in her gold eyes.

"Alton, are you my guardian angel?" Eloise gazed up as if she believed I could give her life.

TWELVE

That night we sat on the emerald-green sofa in my small living room that looked out on the bay. Between the railroad tracks and the black water, the steel tanks of Cascade Cold Storage glittered under the spotlights that lit the empty yards. A freight train bore down along the shore, shaking the hill the Bluestone sat on. Eloise got up and went to the window.

Earlier I'd asked her what she remembered, and she'd told me about a world before the stories. To her, Emily's stories weren't a life, but lines she had to read as an actress reads a hated part. In fact, she saw her commerce with her creator as forced labor. Trying to please Emily had made her ill. Her years with the Vegetarian League, the poignant misunderstanding that turned her into a double agent for the FBI, her life with her lovers and that Dink Merlin—all these were inane, insane imaginings of her book lady.

Emily was a warp in the mold, she said. She (Eloise) didn't like being stoned, nor did she find being stoned, thinking she was a lizard, a very inspiring way to spend her time. She'd never take five lovers. Her oriental jacket was tacky, she'd said, taking it off and throwing it on the floor.

Answering my questions in a factual way I appreciated, Eloise vowed she knew nothing about Emily's missing jacket or Meg's missing drawing. When I asked if the oriental jacket had been Emily's, she (Eloise) got up and said cordially, "Gotta split now, Alton. Places to go."

And just like that she sailed out my door.

I went back to rereading the stories. I called Emily but got no answer. When I reached Thelma, she didn't know where Emily was. I was ready to call the cops and turn myself in when my door opened and Eloise stood there, smiling as if she'd never left.

Where *were* you?" I asked.

She didn't answer, walking over to stand by my window. A flicker of impersonal interest crossed her face as if she, coming from a more beautiful world, saw lights on the water and car chases in reverse as a batch of pleasurable yet meaningless phenomena.

"Do the others remember where they came from?" I didn't know what to call her cohorts from the stories.

"No, they don't, and it's weird." She turned from the window. "When I told them, they said I was, you know—" She made a corkscrew motion beside her ear. "They're creeps."

I loved her direct way of talking, her late-Sixties charm. "What's the first thing you remember?" I asked, kicking idly at frayed tassels on my worn oriental carpet.

In her scratchy voice, tinged with nostalgia, she said, "There was a lake. And songs and stories in the afternoon. It was summer. We had goats. I can't remember any first thing." She sighed. "The only other thing.... It was winter. The lake was frozen. Two grown-ups were pulling me on skates. Wooden runners, you know? They swung me in the air, and that was all. I was so surprised."

"It sounds like a dream," I said. "Did Emily give you dreams of flying?"

"Don't mention that woman," Eloise said in a flat, indignant tone. "And why do you take her side? Maybe I gave *her* the idea."

She squinted down her nose, as if she thought I should get busy and send her back to her world. She turned to the window in a regal, sweeping way. I got up. The sparse lights out by Goosebery Point and the few lights halfway up the hill of Lummi Island glittered over the cold, black water.

"It's not fair to make me take sides. Emily's my friend, too." I kicked at the carpet.

When I said "friend," Eloise smiled. I didn't know why. I glanced down at the pages, as if they held an answer. She was looking around at my unpacked boxes, the rocks on my bureau, what was left of them.

"Do you like living here, Alton?"

I shook my head. Through the glass doors, on a bureau next to the bed, rested my obsidian, gleaming dully like a piece of a black panther's shoulder, princely though a bit dusty.

"Why don't you come with me to the lake? There's room for one more." Her gold-flecked eyes met mine.

My heart pounded. I knew "one more" didn't mean an exclusive arrangement or even my being one of her satellite lovers. I didn't know what I'd be. In the stories, her men friends had been lovers who'd metamorphosed, reforming along the banded lines of friendship.

"Is the lake where you went this afternoon?"

Eloise nodded. "I'm helping out with a wedding. The Dink's friend Caesar." She glanced down at Emily's pages dispassionately, as if freed from their spell.

Emily had told me Caesar was a "sweetie," or his real-life referent was. Me, I didn't know.

"I'll come with you, Eloise."

She smiled. "Okay," she said leisurely, as if she knew the future would take care of itself since she'd planted the seed of a good idea. She stood, one hand on her hip, exuding ease.

"I've never met anyone like you," I blurted out.

"I'm just a person."

For the first time in a while, there wasn't that dry wind in my bones. Something more real was building, flexing and spreading, knitting me together more intricately.

"You're beautiful, Eloise."

She made a face, as if to say, "So what?" And she gave me a level look, as if she were a meadow, wishing to be praised for fruitfulness rather than beauty. Then she grinned, her cheeks round and full, and she laughed her up-on-stilts laugh, the likes of which I hadn't heard since that day on Holly Street.

Turning, she went through the glass door to my bedroom. My bed was unmade. She picked up the obsidian from my bureau and came back through the glass doors. "It's heavy." She hefted it. "You study these things?"

"Not obsidian *per se*. Sedimentary rocks are my department. I don't go out in the field much, except as an unofficial rockhound." I glanced up, and she was still there. "Obsidian, yes, it's igneous. Forms from molten rock—magma that cools fast at the earth's surface. If the pressure cooker bakes the stuff longer at depth, presto, it's a totally new rock."

As my heart thumped, I wondered what she'd think of plate tectonics—continents floating like rafts, contorting seafloors, and plowing up mountains.

"You've seen this?" Eloise asked incredulously, as if I were some plutonic magician who knew the right temperature and pressure to send her back to her world.

"No, but other men have." I thought of the sea-floor spreading at the Mid-Atlantic Ridge that the paleomagicians had measured.

I didn't care for something in her smile.

"Eloise, we assume what's happened once can happen again millions of times. That's the principle of uniformitarianism. The present's the key to the past."

"And to the future?" A hopeful light glowed in her eyes.

"Yes, prediction is the scientist's crowning accomplishment." A supple tension spread through me, interbedding with a part of myself buried too long.

"What do you predict for me?" she asked, taking my hand. We sat down on the couch.

I knew I couldn't predict much about people; recent events had taught me that. "I don't know."

"You don't?" She still gripped the black rock. "I bet you could send me back if you tried, Alton. I get the feeling you know who I am, what I am. You know?"

"You mean, I know your essence?" I asked carefully.

"Yes." She smiled, handing me the obsidian as if it were a gleaming irreducible lump of herself.

Just a little while ago, I'd all but given up on being in a story, and now here was Eloise, asking me to translate her out of one. Her leg brushed mine.

"But something's changed. I'm not the same," she said sadly.

"To me you're the same person you've always been— before the stories, during the stories."

"And now?" she asked softly.

I nodded.

"You'll do it, then? You'll help me?"

I nodded again. She shifted and resettled herself on the couch, but as if unsure of her distances, she bumped me. "Oops." She laughed. Shivering, she hugged herself.

"Are you cold?"

"No. Not that."

"Are you hungry?" Maybe some smoked oysters.

"No." Sighing, she rested one hand on mine. "I'm shaking with desire." She bowed her head, neither shy nor bold, but pleased she'd identified the phenomenon.

In the stories, her way of declaring herself to her lovers was a heartfelt "Let's fuck." I found her facts about having the shivers just as alluring, and I put my arms around her. We kissed. She tasted like cigarettes, but I didn't care. She drew back. The lights in her gold-flecked eyes weren't in the centers, but at the edges, as if something threatened to send her veering off any second.

"Eloise, you're so—" I paused. "Risky to me," I stammered.

"You are to me, too."

The strands of her light-brown hair lay in a feckless way across her forehead. We kissed again.

She drew back. "Shit, I forgot my B.C."

"Your what?"

To me, B.C. meant "Before Clarissa."

"My birth control." Sounding indignant, she reached down and started ransacking her denim shoulder bag on the floor. Soon crumpled sketches, packs of cigarettes, ornate wooden boxes, and rolls of film flew over Emily's pages. Could a mortal man make love with a woman from a story? *Please God, let her be the same species as me.*

She turned the bag upside down. "Damn, I didn't use to need B.C."

"How do you know you need it now?" I was curious.

"Let's not get into a philosophical discussion. I'm here. I probably need it." She got up and stepped over a pile of Emily's pages. "Shit, I don't feel like going out."

"I'll go," I offered.

"No, I'm not letting you." She sat down beside me on the couch, resting her hand on my shoulder.

"But without your B.C.?" I glanced at my hunk of obsidian. Clarissa and I always said we were each other's children.

"Commere, Alton." She took my hand and pulled me to my feet, leading me to my bedroom. The word "commere" was so lovely.

Light shone through the glass doors, her face in shadow. She gave me that level look, still exuding ease. As I looked into her eyes, I remembered her favorite thing was what Emily called "the gold light that lies on highways and long fields in late afternoon." Eloise's way of putting it was "slanted light." She was so direct.

She came closer, brushing my thigh with her knee, nudging me. "Lie down, Alton."

I did, and she knelt on the bed beside me, unbuttoning her white blouse. She dropped it on the floor, took off jeans and underclothes.

"Now you," she said.

I took off my clothes.

She had a swimmer's body, big-shouldered, big-thighed. Her breasts were small and full. In her measured way, she gazed at me out of her wide-set eyes. I moved slowly, as if drugged, or as if the honey color of her eyes had gone into my bones and made me dopey.

Getting up, she went through the glass doors into the kitchen. She came back with two glasses and a pint of Drambuie. I sat up, pressing my back against the cool wall. She walked slowly, padding over my threadbare carpet in a graceful way that belied her big buttocks and hips.

Stammering, I said, "You move so—" She moved in a honey-colored way. I couldn't say that. And then I did.

"That's sweet, Alton," she said, sitting down, pouring out the Drambuie and handing me a glass. The sheets of my unmade bed were gritty. A highway wreck I once saw flashed into my mind. A truck carrying a load of molasses had overturned and road crews hosed down the asphalt for hours.

Heart pounding, I murmured, "You're my honey-pot." I'd heard that somewhere, though I didn't know what it meant.

"That's not very flattering." She cupped the small bulge at her middle. "I'm fat. She made me fat." Glaring at me, she said, "So that's what happens when you get to be almost—thirty?"

She sounded unsure of her facts. She hadn't been thirty in the stories, not even close.

"You're beautiful," I said.

"I'm not. I feel like I'm pregnant, but I can't be pregnant. I haven't done it with anyone *here*."

She said "here" with a rising note of exasperation, and I wanted to ask where "here" was. When I reached out, she pulled away, got up, and flicked off the light. Outside, the sulphur arc light cast its stark, orange light through the window. She drew the shade.

"Damn her," said Eloise. "My body's swelling up on me, stewing in its juices."

"I love you," I said.

She looked past me. "Shit, shit, I never should've come here."

My eyes opened wide. If she said "here" one more time, we'd go up in smoke. *I won't sleep tonight. I'll stay up and watch her.* I pressed the heel of my hand against the nape of her neck. I drew her to me, but she didn't budge.

I wanted to press my lips to her belly, taste her and know what she was like. Was she salty as real people are, or did she taste as honey-colored as she looked? She'd never tell me, as Clarissa had, that we were in hell.

As she kissed my neck and chest, I lay back. My head rested next to her thigh. I was hard. In the light from the window, she was big. I wondered, can she read my thoughts? Maybe I should take ten slugs of that Drambuie.

Bending sideways, she captured the tip of my penis in her mouth. I gasped, drew a breath, closed my eyes. I opened them wide. She was still there. Her small, brown-tipped breasts swayed slightly. I kept closing my eyes and opening them, as if I couldn't decide how best to spend my time.

She was licking me softly, moving up and down. I lay back and let go, as if a cheering section of cherubim were lifting me off the earth. The least I could do was be ready to levitate.

"Stay with me, Eloise!" I cried.

Then I got an idea. "Lie down with me," I said, reaching my arm around her hip.

She tried to rearrange herself, then seemed to change her mind. She kept going. I was about to go sky-high. I rested my hands on her shoulders as she rocked above me. An urgent turning told me what happened next was out of my control. Holding tight, I took a deep breath, bucked my body up, came with a yell, and started having a coughing attack, choking as if my windpipe had been stuffed with cotton.

Gasping, I yelled, "You're my fresh air." My eyes watered, and I wagged my head from side to side, as if my neck weren't working right.

"Are you okay?" she asked, coming up for air. "I haven't done this before. Not really."

I didn't know what "not really" meant.

She rested one hand on my leg as if to steady me. I went on coughing. She got up and turned on the light, poured a few fingers of Drambuie, and handed me the glass. I let the sweet liqueur go down my throat like gold smoke.

She sat on the edge of the bed, a strangely serious look on her face. I wasn't coughing as badly, but I hadn't stopped coughing, either. Tears ran down my face. I felt more real and more embarrassed than I'd ever felt before.

I took a few more sips, then put the glass down. I drew her to me, bent over, tried to press my lips to her belly. She pushed me away.

"You don't want me to?" I asked, astonished.

She smiled and shook her head.

Clarissa and I had an excellent sex life, I'd thought—if not as rapturous as our farewell in the vault, and not as awkward as our first time sixteen years ago—still our hallmark had been equity. Now it seemed to me our passion had been like currency we exchanged, as we discussed the bargain we'd struck. Watching each other as if from either end of a seesaw, waving and making signs like third-base coaches, we measured who gave more and who gave less, adjusting our signals for the next session.

"What about your pleasure, Eloise?"

"I got pleasure."

As she gazed at me out of her gold eyes, I felt an endless slate had been wiped clean. The six months of scenes in the vault hadn't happened. The sixteen years of Stevens and my wife doing whatever they did, however infrequently, hadn't happened either. The Dying Warrior could think about them if he wanted to. I didn't care.

As I stared into Eloise's innocent yet ancient eyes, I felt wonder. It was as if I'd been sunk into an abyss. *She's made of light. Her world is made of light. If I lay my hand on her side, it'll go right through her.*

Eloise sipped her Drambuie soberly, as if the drink had cleared her head. Me, I was ready to get dizzier.

☦

Though I didn't stay up all night and watch her sleep, neither did she disappear. Toward dawn, I woke, rolled over, sat up. In the pale light that came from the kitchen, Eloise sat on the living-room floor, reading Emily's rough drafts.

"Damn her, damn her," she muttered.

To Eloise the pages were the emblems of a paltry existence where she was pulled on strings by a woman who wrote what she did for her own purposes—a name, or maybe escape.

"Poignant misunderstanding, my ass," Eloise quoted mockingly. "She's going to pay."

I stumbled into the living room and stood there. Eloise sat in a sea of white paper. She was my soul come back to me, the proof of my madness, and she hated her creator, my friend.

"You know where she is, don't you, Eloise?"

Letting the pages fall, she smiled.

THIRTEEN

Under a dawn that blew in tatters off the smoky hills, we raced uphill toward the lake. The bass guitar of "Green Onions" boomed on the radio. Leaning into a curve, Eloise drummed the heel of one hand on the steering wheel. In the back seat, her blue satin oriental jacket lay crumpled on top of Emily's box of pages. My throat was hot and dry.

Eloise's news about her friends at the lake hadn't been inspiring. They'd been laughing about some big score the Dink had made—I thought maybe it was his beloved Maui Wowie—but Eloise said the Burger King wrappers she'd found stashed in the saddlebags of his Honda Golden Glide were a dead giveaway. She didn't care if the Golden Glide was a clean and powerful machine. Nor did she care if the Dink did have the Secretary of Agriculture on ice and fifteen million beneficial insects ready to do the bidding of the Vegetarian League. She knew something he didn't.

"Is Emily okay?" I remembered the black-helmetted Dink on the motorcycle roaring away from her apartment. "*Is* she?"

"I think so, dammit."

I didn't think now was the best time to mention my thoughts on the subject of marriage, nor of our making a side trip to the pharmacy near the Miracle to get some B.C.

Clearly, Eloise's attitude toward her creator wasn't the best. And when my own poor parents had telephoned just as we were about to leave the Bluestone, briefly Eloise hadn't seemed happy with me, either.

"Can't wait to—"

"Sea-Tac, flight 463—"

"So glad to—"

"Roger and out—"

My father and mother, it seemed, were coming on the next plane. Talking like a great, two-headed being on their two extensions, as was their custom, they chose not to hear my pleas that now wasn't the best time for a family reunion. As the familiar voices streamed across the continent, I smiled at Eloise, mouthing the word "parents," but she tapped her foot and frowned. My longing was mixed with a strange regret. As I signed off, she picked up Emily's box of pages. "We're taking them," she announced in a flat tone.

Now as the Valiant swung around a curve, the sun came out, and the lake opened, long and straight, glinting dully, as if it had just been scoured by the glacier in Wisconsinian time, 14,000 years ago. Humming "Green Onions," only a bit off-key, Eloise moved her body to the music. The sun lit the light-brown fuzz on her forearms. Squinting, she bunched up her black T-shirt and scratched her shoulder. I lay my hand lightly on it.

So what if Emily wasn't crazy about the idea of putting me in a story? Seeing Eloise and me together would bring her around. So what if the redoubtable Dink Merlin did come back? If he laid a hand on Eloise, I'd send him to the Precambrian—if need be, Emily's non-husband, her correspondent from Monroe Prison, and a host of innocent bystanders, too.

It hit me that Eloise hadn't made any forays into reverse today. Nor had she disappeared. Maybe I was having a steadying effect. I gave her shoulder a squeeze. In reply, she flashed me a grin like that of a child, purely happy, set free after a long illness. The Valiant tilted on two wheels. The lake went up, and a jolt of wonder shot from my hips to my solar plexus.

After only a few wrong turns, we pulled onto a gravel road at the south end of the lake. Sandstone boulders and glacial outwash littered the shore. In a field of trucks and weeds, half-hidden behind heaps of warped boards and piles of fish net tangled like great spider webs, stood a brown house with its windows knocked out. It was the same house Emily and I had looked at, north of town, on Enterprise Road. Now here it was, thirteen miles south of town, sitting on a concrete-block foundation like a statue with broken eyes. A chill went up my back.

"I've seen this house," I said.

"Me too, damn her."

Maybe Eloise meant she remembered something of her life as Emily's sister Meg. This was, after all, the house where they once lived. Maybe Emily had to remember, too, before she could forgive and forget.

A bald young man with thick long arms and a serene smile on his simian face burst out of the house like a man in a cartoon going through a wall. Cradling a rifle in the crook of one arm, he beamed at Eloise, then casually took me in, as if I were some low-level adjunct to the Secretary of Agriculture.

I grasped Eloise's elbow, but she shook free. "Meet my friend, Caesar," she said.

He nodded, as if any friend of Eloise were entitled to his good cheer, and he propped the gun on one shoulder. The Dink, he informed us, was off doing his appointed rounds.

"By the way," Caesar added mildly, in a deep, soft voice, "we've got the freaking Secretary—"

"You've what?" I stepped forward. I couldn't believe Eloise and her friends had kidnapped the man. It was all right to read about such things. But to go and *do* it?

"He's not a he. He's a she," said Caesar, scratching one huge, bare arm. "She's a bit tied up, you might say." He laughed immensely at his little joke.

Just visible between firs and cedars, the lake shone dully. A low sky hugged the dark hills. Eloise started toward the house, going past a dying garden that hadn't been turned under: four drooping sunflowers, three rows of cornstalks, a few pumpkins, and some rows of leafy things that had gone to seed.

"Is this—" I could've sworn it was Emily's garden.

"Courtesy of our friend, Merlin," said Caesar, ho-ho-ing like a bald, burly benefactor. "The old hocus-pocus, by George, I think the Dink's really got it. No blood, sweat, and tears." He laughed uproariously, then told us the Secretary had been filling up on the Dink's Maui Wowie cookies and Grand Marnier liqueur, her new health food diet, he said, so she could get the show on the road.

"What's he talking about?" I glanced at Eloise, who was heading inside. Politely, Caesar tipped the rifle my way, and we went in.

In a long, bare room, whose one piece of furniture was a threadbare blue sofa, sat Emily Weed. Her arms were tied behind her, feet bound. She wore an embroidered silver gown that resembled a flapper's wedding dress.

She took one look at Eloise, and her warm hazel eyes opened wide. Emily burst into tears, let out a cry, coughed, swallowed, and went on coughing.

"Oh, Meg, no." Her eyes wet, full of disbelief and wonder, she gazed at Eloise, who regarded her creator coolly. In a yearning voice, racked by coughs, Emily repeated, "No, no."

I remembered when I'd showed her the drawing of Eloise. Emily had gotten that same pained, rapt look. She'd been so frightened when I'd told her I'd seen Eloise outside the Salvation Army Store. Now she wept. Shaking her head slowly, she murmured reverently, "You took everything,

Meg." She stuck out her small chin bravely. "Why'd you have to—why'd I make you—leave?"

Eloise stood, arms crossed, exuding ease. "What's this Meg shit?" she demanded in a level tone, facing me, one fist on her hip. As she gazed at me out of her gold eyes, bright with her impersonal brand of mirth and good cheer, our night in the Bluestone seemed to open up and hang between us, gorgeous as the Grand Canyon. Emily let out another rasping cough.

"What's this thing you two have with coughing fits?" demanded Eloise, standing squarely, looking dead at me.

My face was hot. "Uh, Eloise, please—"

"Look, he's blushing." Eloise grinned at her creator in an almost companionable way.

"You *slept* with her, didn't you, Alton?" wailed Emily. She tugged at her ropes. She groaned, coughed, cleared her throat, and spat.

"Yuck, gross," said Eloise.

Emily was crying. "I knew it, Meg. And you, damn you to hell, Alton Broome, you unreasonable maggot! My own sister, who I never—we never even got to—say *goodbye*." She was trying to enunciate in her clipped, nasal tones, but she slurred her words.

"Jesus, am I stoned." Emily's eyes were glassy and dilated. She tugged at her ropes, the tendons in her neck showing. She gave me a hurt look.

Eloise was squinting at me like a funky rebel angel, as if she thought I could try harder to keep up my end of this conversation. I pressed my fingers to my forehead and dug in my nails. I wanted to rip off my Rock of Ages face—it felt stuck like the Dying Warrior's grimace.

"Can't we untie her?" I asked in a low voice.

Eloise shook her head. Caesar guffawed.

"I'm untying her," I announced, stepping forward.

"Look, Alton," said Eloise, cocking her head, "you can't back out."

Caesar pointed the rifle my way, ho-hoed, and shook his huge, pink head. "We've got big plans for you and the Secretary. Oh, my aching back, tomorrow and tomorrow, and so forth." He stopped, as if awed by his words. "It must be happening again," he muttered.

"Why's Emily a prisoner?" I asked pointedly.

"Don't you get it?" Eloise all but stamped her foot. "We're making her finish." She sounded tired. "We've got her, and we've got...." She draped one arm across my shoulder.

Eloise couldn't mean *me*. "But I thought you wanted to go back." I was frightened. I didn't fancy being added insurance, the paleomagician on loan.

Shaking, I glanced from Eloise to Emily and back again, remembering how I used to carry messages between my parents on their barricades. "You two ladies have some issues to discuss," I said loudly, booming like my father.

Emily laughed. Eloise pulled her arm back from my shoulder. "I'm not talking to her."

"Me neither." Emily pressed her lips together. "She's no lady, Alton, I can tell you that."

Both women glared at me. Emily pulled herself erect and threw back her head, seeming tall though she was sitting.

"So Meg, you're back to haunt us one more time." Emily spoke in her nasal, accusing tone, as if she were a royal personage, used to being addressed in the first-person plural. She stuck out her small chin.

Eloise stuck out her own chin, squinting. They were both fierce—Eloise, gold-eyed, rocking on her heels; Emily, thinner, darker, and so real.

"Look at her, Alton, she's glaring *down* at me," said Emily, complaining like an older sister whose height or age had never been respected. She bowed her head slightly. She sniffed. Her eyes were wet. I wanted to dry them. I moved toward the couch, but Caesar laughed, slapping his thigh.

Eloise was frowning. "She always lorded it over me, Alton. Miss Queen of the Manor."

"Oh, I did not," said Emily.

"Shut up, you book lady. Bag lady's more like it." Eloise spat out her words, sticking her nose in Emily's face.

"I'll call you what I like." Emily sounded smug. "I know when to call a spade a spade." Tugging at her ropes, she shouted, "And I'll call it a bloody shovel if I want to!"

Emily turned to me triumphantly, smiling as if she'd proved some point to her satisfaction. She hiccupped. "Alton, they've been making me eat all this Maui Wowie and all this ice cream, too. I'm gonna be so fat I'll get cancer. My wrinkles'll get cancer. Shit, shit."

Emily's voice had risen to a wail. Bowing slightly, she frowned in that way I'd never liked and said softly, as if she'd known her sister's ghost would disappoint her, "Oh, Meg, how could you?"

Eloise stared at her with amazement, then glanced at me, shaking her head. "Tell her, Alton."

"What does she mean, she isn't Meg?" Emily's voice was accusing. She straightened her shoulders, face red and blotchy. "Tell her it's not fair for her to haunt me and pretend she isn't Meg."

"I'm *Eloise*, and I'm here to make trouble!" my heroine shouted.

Emily's shoulders sagged, and her head slumped. Her eyes rolled woozily under her eyelids.

Scared, I glanced around this big, bare room, its walls a dirty yellow. Smoke drifted in through broken windows. A goat bleated. Fir trees pressed closer. Tapping her foot, Eloise hummed the bass notes of "Green Onions." Caesar had a penitent look on his lovesick face. Damn his bald head and huge arms.

"You got it all wrong," Eloise was saying. "I'd never treat that fisherman in Alaska like that. I'd never carry dental floss taped to my wrist, goddamn it, like a hospital I.D. bracelet. I hate hospitals. I hate plastic. It's environmentally unsound."

Emily jerked to attention. "I never said anything about I.D. bracelets."

"But I did." I remembered how I'd once compared Eloise's band of dental floss to a hospital bracelet, Clarissa's.

Emily frowned. Eloise steamed on, working herself into a fury. "If a man cooked chocolate mousse for me, I'd do dishes."

"Sure, sure," said Emily. "You never did them. Ask her, Alton. When we lived together, I used to pile up her dishes in her room as a little reminder."

"I'm not Meg. I'm Eloise!"

Her words seemed torn out of me. My bones were made of smoke. When Eloise looked at me for confirmation, in triumph, I knew that if she asked me, I'd go with her, declare myself her paleomagician forever. The bare room in the dark house floated over the lake. Emily was gazing at me out of her soft, warm eyes.

"This is a side issue!" shouted Eloise. "I'm tired of doing scenes this way and that way, every time you feel it. And you—you never finish—you just leave us hanging. You made me sick. I'm grotesque. It's like I'm pregnant, but I can't be pregnant, can I?"

Taking my arm, she announced, "It's gonna be different now."

I stared into Eloise's gold eyes.

"I'd never take six lovers, Alton!" Her scratchy voice was pointblank and cold.

"Five," Emily insisted, "I never gave her more than five. Tell her, Alton." She looked at me in a dazed, muffled way.

"She's right, Eloise," I said, aghast at being the court of last appeal. My voice sounded thin, querulous, like my mother's. What was happening to me?

"Five, shmive!" Eloise yelled. "I'd never be caught dead carrying a saddle in the middle of New York. I hate New York. I hate Bob Dylan. I hate folk music. It's history. It's toast. And—" She looked at Emily— "I hate *you!*"

Glaring at her creator, Eloise broke into tears. I groaned.

Emily gazed past Eloise, past me, and in my mind I was walking down Diamond Street late at night, Emily a vague figure behind white curtains.

"I wouldn't get lost in the Metropolitan," Eloise was saying, wiping her eyes roughly with the back of one hand. "I know every inch of it."

"How do you know it?" asked Emily softly, clipping her words precisely, smiling her lost-cause smile.

"Because *you* know it," Eloise hissed.

"You can read her mind?" I asked, amazed.

"Alton, I'm no eavesdropper. That'd be tacky. I just know some of her thoughts, well, 'cause she gave them to me. I know how old she is and how many pounds overweight she is."

I raised an eyebrow. That wasn't a fact.

Turning, Eloise pointed almost rudely and shouted, "I know it's over, you and your non-husband. You're just bouncing on the rebound to old Alton here."

What did she mean, "old Alton"? And Emily and I were just friends.

Eloise flashed me a gleam of her impersonal regard, tinged with amusement. Turning to Emily, she squinted as if at a bright light.

"I'm Eloise," she said, her flat, disgusted tone almost too familiar, as if she were asking who else would kidnap such an obscure writer.

Emily wept. Her shoulders shook.

Eloise went on. "By the way, we didn't sleep together, you snoop. We just—" She tossed off a laugh, and I thought of the first time I saw her on Holly Street. Now her laugh was different, a scratchy, angelic battle cry. She was different. I wished I'd had more of her fury when I'd had my little chat with Stevens.

"Spare us the details," Emily muttered.

Both women looked at me—Emily bravely, hopefully, all but calling out to me as if to a befuddled genie. I was going to have to choose between Emily and this fierce figment squaring her shoulders.

My rib cage felt as if it were being subducted by some ancient seafloor. Outside, over the trees, the clouds lay on top of the hills like a frozen wave.

A wan, crooked smile pulled down one corner of Emily's mouth. If ever there were a lost cause, this was it. The two women would never get together. I'd never be in a story. Eloise would disappear, or we'd end up in prison or the Bin, and right when my parents were coming, too.

A dry wind seeped through my bones from four billion years ago. I was a disloyal monster.

I glanced from Eloise to her creator like a man at a tennis match between two whimsical deities. I didn't know what password applied. I was worse than a monster. I could save no one. The dry wind had become colder. A part of my chest cavity seemed to rip loose, like a rifted margin. The hills came closer. I tried to picture Eloise sitting on the curb of Commercial Street or riding her white horse covered with leeches. I couldn't.

I let out a long, rising cry. "Emily, I'm sorry." I was ready to go on saying I was sorry to my students I'd abandoned, Clarissa whom I hadn't saved, and my poor mother and father I hadn't written in weeks.

"Eloise, you're so mean to her!" I cried.

For a second, Emily closed her eyes. There was a loud buzzing. We looked around us. Eloise seemed to grow older. I thought I saw a few strands of gray in her hair. I glanced away. Next to the blue couch, under a wall with Meg's drawing of the three women, stood Emily's desk. Where had it come from? On the desk sat Emily's typing paper, her typewriter, her box of crayons. Beside the desk was a tall metal filing cabinet, a hunk of Stevens' shield rock on top.

Eloise and Caesar glanced at these new additions, then at me. "Oh, right, I knew that," said Caesar excitedly, his pink face gleaming. "The Dink said we were supposed to get those, too."

Emily gazed at me imploringly.

"It's been a long time, Alton," said Eloise.

Hadn't I once said those words?

"I knew it, if we got them together." Eloise all but clapped her hands.

"She's not the Secretary of Agriculture, is she?" asked Caesar sadly.

Eloise shook her beautiful head. This was insane. I was insane. That's why Eloise had a hospital I.D. bracelet. Clarissa and her three competent therapists would work on us cheek to cheek.

Eloise ran out of the room. In a second, she tore back in, carrying the box of Emily's pages. She set it down at my feet, pulled out her rumpled oriental jacket, and tossed it on the floor. She yanked a page from the top of the pile. Holding it close to her eyes, she squinted as she moved her lips with the words.

"Shit, she made me dyslexic," Eloise said, holding out the page to me, almost shyly.

"You thief!" wailed Emily. "You took my pages. Alton, I told you when something's over, it's over."

"We rescued them," said Eloise, giving me a loving look. My lips trembled.

Smiling, Eloise took the page and waltzed over to Emily's side. Haltingly, she read the words, "Chapter One, by, um, Alton Broome." She grinned. "Um, Once I was a reasonable man." Turning to Caesar, she cried out, "I knew it. She's been holding out on us."

I gazed at Emily, stunned. The buzzing stopped. The words Eloise had read sounded familiar. They sounded like me, but I couldn't remember saying them. They were the truth about me, and I wanted her to go on reading.

Eloise knelt beside me, wetting her lips, flipping through yellow, handwritten, legal-size pages as if they were banknotes. She pulled one out. "Here, Alton. You like to read," she said, smiling.

Emily's protest sounded far away.

Painfully, I read aloud: "I stuck my tongue out, testing the glass. I pulled it back in. Was it Puget Sound I tasted?"

In black and white, too real, was the day I'd licked my message onto the window at Clarissa's and my old house.

I groaned. I'd wanted to be in a story that was funny or uplifting. But this was awful. This was my life. This was real.

"Alton," said Eloise calmly, "meet your...creator."

I stared at my bound friend.

"And you, book lady, meet your whatchamacallit—"

"My narrator? Really?" Emily sounded aghast, yet she gazed at me fondly. "Jesus, I really am stoned." She said the word "really" with a rising note of wonder, and I thought of when we ran down her street chasing pages.

I dug out pages from Emily's box. What had been drafts of stories from *Yes, I Don't Love You, Merlin* was now a set of neat pages, told by yours truly, but not in my handwriting. One chapter was titled, "In and Out of the Vault With Alton."

I let out a moan. "Emily, I told you my secrets." So she had been looking for material after all.

Emily bowed her head. One corner of her mouth seemed to go up; one went down. I guess you could say she smiled.

"Could I...?" Emily paused, staring intently. "Can I see that stuff a second, Alton?"

I shoved my—our?—treatise on tongues and windows in her face.

"Hmm, not bad." Emily gave a little grin. "But Alton, all I wrote was the stuff about you and your window." She shook her head, blushing.

"It's her handwriting, isn't it, Alton?" asked Eloise.

"But I didn't write it," Emily wailed. "Just that one teensy-weensy scene." She was crying. "I couldn't help it. It wasn't my fault." Then she hiccupped.

Did she mean her hiccups or her writing? "But you said you stopped writing," I said in disbelief.

"I didn't stop thinking about you, Alton. It was just one little scene."

I didn't care for the way she said "little."

"I thought you wanted this, Alton." Emily bit off her words precisely. Her eyes had no warmth, a field gone dry. If she could have raised an arm, she'd have made her waving, qualifying gesture.

"You could've told me, Emily."

"And you could've had a real woman, not a story." Emily gave me her sad smile.

This can't be real, I thought. I tried hitting my head; it hurt.

"Shit, I always knew she was sweet on you," said Eloise. Facing her creator—and mine?—she demanded, "No more writing it in your head." So that was why Eloise kept disappearing. "Now finish it, or else—"

Eloise's eyes glinted crazily. Caesar aimed the rifle at me, cocking it, smiling in an unfriendly way.

I calculated the distance. Maybe Emily was right. Eloise did use people. But what about Emily? She hadn't been straightforward with me, either.

"I told you you'd be disappointed, Alton," said Emily softly. Disappointed with *Eloise*, I'd thought she meant.

"Emily, write *The End!*" I cried.

Emily's eyes, unfocused, gazed past me. Her ropes came loose, and she rubbed her wrists. As a motorcycle roared, I turned to Eloise. But she was gone. She and Caesar were gone.

Outside, a light moved over the water. "Eloise!" I cried out.

She was so far away—such small, white spaces.

Emily stood up, held out her arms. To me? To *her*?

I bumped into Stevens' file cabinet, threw open the door, and staggered out past a pickup truck, weeds growing out of its half-raised hood. I tore through brush, banged my head on a branch. I had spider webs in my mouth. Gasping, I stood on the shore.

A reddish haze, reflecting the lights of town, shone over the hills, the black water.

I plunged in, dove down, trailed my fingers in weeds and muck. "I'll save you, Eloise!" I cried.

I was underwater, someone grasping at my heels.

I was back by the bay where Eloise had saved me. Teeth chattering, I stood in chest-deep water, staring at humpbacked Lummi Island looming like a sea beast or some huge glacial erratic. I dove, came up, and dove again.

I felt the pull of sediment, of dark water.

Eloise and I, we'd skitter in the substrate with the spider crab, jellyfish, and sea worm, go down through the grains of the ages, the layers of deep time.

I gulped in water. There was a ringing in my ears.

☦

When I came to, I was coughing, shivering. My chin lay in the sand, and my feet trailed in the water. I got up on one elbow. Dark hills, a reddish glow in the sky.

My throat ached. My mouth tasted like pond scum. I cupped some water, wet my lips. It wasn't salt. I was at the lake. And I remembered:

Emily had been holding out her arms.

Blurred images interbedded. "Cretaceous, Ordovician," I muttered, trying to remember....

I was underwater, someone grasping at my heels.

And before that, I'd been running.

Devonian, Silurian.

There'd been a motorcycle, and....

Dink Merlin came back. He said, "No more stories. I want a novel. Big bucks, cast of thousands, Return of the Dink, *Part Thirteen." He took Emily's red pen and gave it to Eloise. She wrote in her dizzy scrawl....*

The Dink and I were standing over Stevens' body in the house on Grunion Road. Fifteen million beneficial insects made a hive of honey in my ear.

I took a file from Stevens' tall gray cabinet, and I read facts about his drug deals, magic mushrooms, lovers of legal and not-so-legal age. His lovers of both sexes. I groaned.

The Dink laid his hand on my shoulder. He had dirty-yellow eyes.

Eloise started up the Silver-Wraith, Stevens' files in the back seat. "You're one of us, Alton," she said.

The Dink handed me Stevens' poker. It was warm. "No innocent bystanders," he said. "Finish him off."

"Uh, Merlin," said Eloise. "If he finishes him off, we're in deep shit, and we can't get back—"

"Oh, right, I knew that," said the Dink.

I was crying. I was crazy. These shadows were all crazy. I wasn't a murderer. Or a blackmailer....

Miocene, Pleistocene, Eocene.

In a house with no windows, the Dink and Eloise were naked. They kissed. I watched. I was naked. And....

Eloise walked away from me, her big hips slowly rolling. We were in the vault. Eloise had leeches on her neck.

I screamed.

The Dink came toward me, veins sticking out of his skinny arms. And he turned into Stevens. We were in his house. Standing by his shield rock, Stevens held out both hands as if to bless me. Heat haze shimmered up from his mole-headed chess pieces. Stevens bent to kiss me.

I hit him with the poker. Smoke spewed out of a dark bruise on the side of Stevens' head. And....

My father and I were on a cliff. He glued me to my spot, one hand on top of my head. I punched him in the stomach, and we fell off the cliff. And....

Eloise revved us backward in the Valiant.

Layers and more layers, like the ones in the Grand Canyon—Coconino, Bright Angel, Vishnu....

Eloise and I were tied up in the basement of my parents' house. They'd thrown us down a laundry chute.

My folks were a two-headed being, both heads talking at once. They'd always been two-headed.

"Mom, I'm sorry I had to leave home," I said. "Dad, I can't shine your shoes anymore."

"Son, never heard of—"

"Never writes—"

"It's a wedding—"

"A perglomination—"

"Glom the left half onto—"

"Hey, fuck that idea," Eloise broke in. "I'm not getting squeegied onto you, Alton."

"Will you marry me, Eloise?" I cried.

"No, Alton." She sounded sad.

My parents' heads rotated like guns on turrets. Pipes knocked. The boiler growled. The basement was hung with party streamers. My mother's face was tragic....

My folks and I, we were floating undersea. I was digging my dog Landy's grave.... I was handing Emily my notebook. Emily and I were standing in her garden. Something was burning. Yellow flowers grew out of her ankles.

I dove underwater. Someone called my name—a Slavic, guttural voice that sounded like Clarissa's mother.

Her fingernails raked at my heels....

✠

I pulled myself up on both knees and crawled out of the water, my mouth still tasting like pond scum, like the mud when I'd saved Landy. Over the hills, a low moon and dark racing clouds. A motorcycle roared. I staggered back up to the house.

But there was no house.

A concrete-block foundation jutted out of dry weeds hissing in the wind. On the driver's side of the Valiant, stuck to the rim of the window frame, a few shards of broken glass swayed slightly. On the ground beside a pile of fish net lay a torn sleeve of Eloise's blue satin oriental jacket.

I knelt and hid my face in the cool, wet silk. Damn, something sharp. I let go. I got in my car, turned on the dome light, put my hand to my lips. It came away bleeding. A rock, one of my thundereggs, lay in the back seat where Emily's box of pages had been.

Like a dead man, I started up the Valiant.

Fourteen

I tried to crank the Valiant up in reverse, but it wouldn't do more than twenty. I didn't know how Eloise revved it up so high. Cars don't go that fast in reverse, not real ones. I headed down the lake road in fourth gear, pushing sixty, humming "Green Onions." I was crying.

I screeched to a stop on Diamond Street and ran upstairs. The broken lock had been fixed.

"Emily," I called out, pounding on the door.

No answer, but the door creaked open. A light was on. Cardboard boxes labeled *KITCHEN* and *BOOKS* stood in a stack by the door. Her walls and floors were bare— bookshelves empty, bare cupboards in the kitchen. I ran in and threw open a back window, half expecting to see Emily burying pages in her garden. I ran downstairs and went around back. The dead cornstalks, sunflowers, and pumpkins had been cut down, her garden turned under. I took a pinch of soil—it tasted like clay.

Numbly, I drove off. Maybe I hadn't seen Eloise, and we never took those pages to the lake. I'd lost her, and now Emily was moving without even telling me. *Shit, I don't even have Eloise's jacket.*

As I ran up the stairs of the Bluestone, Miss Bosom—my landlady, the woman I'd once mistaken for Eloise—poked her head out her door and said, "Alton, you've had all these messages. Your wife. And a woman named Thelma. And your parents. And these hippies in a VW Bug with 'Brunhilda' painted on it stopped and left you these."

She held out a green spiral notebook—my diary—and a small sheaf of yellow, legal-size, handwritten pages, Emily's pages. "Your earthly effects, she called them."

"Oh, my God, thanks!" I cried, reaching out, my arms full of stories again.

"Was that your Eloise?" Miss Bosom was smiling, her cheeks round as the big E's.

I beamed at her.

She smiled. "I'm happy for you, Alton."

Saying "thank you" over and over, I ran upstairs. *I'm a lucky monster,* I told myself. *I should call my parents. I should call Clarissa and Thelma, too. I should find Emily.* But what I did was sit and read. My old couch did its best to welcome me, as if it had missed me.

I reread Emily's account of my licking the window, also bits and scraps of what seemed to be a memoir about her sister, set at the house on Enterprise Road. And in my notebook, there was my night with Eloise at the Bluestone, our week at the lake. But I wasn't gone a week, and I didn't remember writing this.

Mountains push up and wear back down again.

It was after nine when I got to Enterprise Road. I thought of when Emily and I first drove here and she said Meg wasn't Eloise. Now the dark house loomed like a derelict ship. Windows broken, it was the house from the lake. I shone a flashlight and climbed in, picking my way through broken glass. I bumped my chin against something metallic. Shit. I shone the light on a tall file cabinet, yanked out a file. In the orange glow of my flashlight, I read the neat script of a letter signed, sincerely, by Stevens.

My hair stood on end. I was shaking. I wasn't sure if I'd killed Stevens or not. "Finish him off," Dink Merlin had said. I shuddered. Shining the light, I reread facts about Stevens' lovers of both sexes, about his drug deals. My shadows were true shadows. Panting, I lugged out the files and took off. I stashed them in a mini-storage on the Guide Meridian, jotted down a note in my notebook, and drove to town, hungry for smoked oysters.

✝

I picked up my phone when I hit the Bluestone, but someone was already on the line.

"Emily?" I cried, swallowing the lump in my throat. If I'd let her down in her own story, it wasn't my fault.

"No, it's me, Thelma. Where've you been?"

"Away. Emily's gone. She was kidnapped, and—and I escaped. I was in this story, but now—" I stopped. My voice had sounded staccato, clipped, like Emily's.

Thelma laughed. "Alton, I saw her tonight. She didn't say anything about being kidnapped. Except by her writing. She's back at it. And she said something about a vault. She's been looking for you. And, oh, yes, she's moving soon."

"Where?"

"South end of Lake Whatcom. That old fixer-upper she lived in with her sister, she's having it moved."

I groaned. And then I smiled.

"Alton," said Thelma kindly, "we've been worried. Clarissa called your parents. They're here, at a motel, the New Whatcom. Oh, yes, and Stevens, his place was burglarized, his papers stolen?" Her voice went up. "And your old place, Alton—yours and Clarissa's—there are all these TVs and VCRs on your front porch. There's a new Porsche parked in the driveway. It's like 'Let's Make a Deal.' Have you started a life of crime?"

"He's a prick," I said.

Thelma went on. "This past week, he's been pathetic. He's had this incurable case of hiccups. The roof of his house caved in. His drain field flooded. So did his basement. It's full of these strange, glowing fish. His clay-woman gateposts fell over. He went to his office and smashed his practice piano. He goes around looking for you, asking is this going to be like Pharaoh and the plagues." She laughed her old-world laugh, thin and watery like Clarissa's mother's.

"He's looking for me?" I repeated, astonished. So that was why gifts were piled in front of my old house. If I were a blackmailer, so be it.

"Where's Emily?" I asked, shakily.

"She said something about her non-husband. Seeing him off. He's going back to New York. Too many trees out here, I guess. He's been here a week." She laughed. "I'm not supposed to tell you, but, Alton, she asked when your divorce is going to be final."

"Soon," I said, surprised it felt right to say it.

Thelma sighed, sounding relieved. "She should be at Sea-Tac now, or on her way back. I'll tell her you called. She's staying with me until she moves." Again, she laughed. "Alton, are you there? Oh, yes, Clarissa, she saw the stuff on your porch. She said you're a man of many surprises. You should call her. She was in the hospital. But now she's out. She's with this young body-builder named Caesar. You want her new number?"

I swallowed hard again. I wanted my commerce with shadows to stay on the page.

"You should call her, Alton."

Sighing, I took down Clarissa's number and said goodbye gratefully. *I should call my parents,* I thought.

✣

I let Clarissa's phone ring for a minute. It was after ten, but what the hell. I was in a story.

"Meet me at the vault," I told my wife.

She laughed. "Alton, it's the middle of the night. Banks are closed." I thought she sounded glad I'd called.

"Well, how about the Miracle?" It still rankled that I'd done our wash there all those extra Wednesdays—the first, third, and fifth ones of the month.

"How about Boulevard Park, Alton? It's almost Christmas. There'll be people," she said sadly. "Watching the lights, you know? " She sighed. "You never took the Peking glass or the bone-and-ivory hands or anything."

At the park, dozens of boats with red and green lights rigged for the holiday season floated in the black water. Out past the small craft, a tanker shifted slowly, its running lights rippling through spidery winches. It was almost eleven o'clock, a few clumps of people gazing out.

Clarissa was getting out of her silver BMW. I waved, and she came across the parking lot. Slowly, almost casually, we strolled across the dark lawn past the big cedar stump, and I thought of when Clarissa got out of the hospital and said she'd come so far. Now it was almost as if we'd never met in cubicles number one and three.

"I want a divorce," I said, my voice scratchy as Eloise's. Clarissa could have her jewels; I'd take my rocks, what was left of them. Fifty-fifty, even steven. So what if she'd carted my best rocks to the landfill.

My wife's sad voice came as if from across the water. "We had nice times, didn't we, Alton?"

I nodded, shivered.

"You know I was Back In again?" she asked wryly, touching her face, her hair.

"Thelma told me."

"I had to break with both of you, Alton."

I hugged my jacket around my neck.

"Alton, I saw that stuff on our porch. The rumor is Thelma took his files. You two have something on him, don't you?" She sounded awed, disappointed, scared. "I guess I didn't have to protect you, did I?"

"Is that why you went with him?" I asked, appalled. "Clarissa, no."

She reached out her gloved hand to me, then put it to her mouth. My teeth were chattering. I thought of when she handed me her list of three competent therapists.

"Alton, last month I told him if he didn't tell you, I would." She sighed. "I used to think I went with him for you, to help you. Your career. But that wasn't it. I kept trying to get back to something. You know he saved me once?"

"You talk like he's a god."

"Well, in a way." Her voice trailed off. "We were co-counselors, Alton, when I first came out here."

She'd never told me that. I knew a bit about re-evaluation counseling, just that it was a sort of lay therapy in which clients were supposed to help each other by listening, not advising.

In jagged gasps, her voice shook. "He was...my savior, my persecutor. I was...." She shrugged, grimaced. The lines in her mouth pulled down on one side.

"He didn't mind playing God with you, did he?" Or with me.

Eyes wet, she shrugged as if still offering something. "I did love you, Alton," she said softly.

I turned, and we drifted away from the water. I was a shadow. I'd always been a shadow. When Clarissa and Stevens and I watched that show about reptiles, there were things I'd seen I hadn't wanted to see. If Clarissa created her persecutor, maybe I'd invited Stevens' shabby behavior, too. Funny, I didn't see these things when I wasn't fictional.

A locomotive pulling a load of freight cars urged itself slowly past the warehouses of the Cold Storage Complex. The train was small and black across the water.

"Thanks for telling me," I said.

Her big, mobile face broke into a grateful grin.

We were at her car. I opened the door, and she got in. I was the man in the moon, a man in a story. She drove off, and I stood there as the red taillights dwindled.

✝

"Eloise," I said, as I got back in the Valiant, "if you'd come with me to number one, things could be different." I thought of Clarissa and Caesar, slammed my fist against the steering wheel, let out a yell. My hand ached. And Emily said stories couldn't change things. Why wasn't she here to tell me what to do? She was lolligagging in Seattle, seeing off her non-husband. A likely story.

At the Bluestone, I pulled the Dying Warrior out of my closet where it sat on top of Emily's pages. I put on the mask and dialed Stevens' number.

"You sent me the Porsche, didn't you?" I demanded shakily.

"Ah, Alton, my little token of good faith." Stevens' dry voice sounded almost friendly. He hiccupped, then cursed softly.

"I don't want your major appliances. Or your Porsche." *Sorry, Eloise.* "I want you to leave me and Clarissa alone."

"Alton, I'm aggrieved you took my files." He hiccupped. "I could let bygones—I mean, we could be friends."

"We were never friends, you—you pharaoh." I'd meant to call him a fucker, but that's what came out.

"Alton." He paused, chuckling. "This pharaoh's fucked more women than you ever have."

I felt a dry wind in the back of my knees.... *We were back in Stevens' house. He was coming toward me, my ears filled with bees, as he bent to force a kiss on me.*

I tightened the phone wire around my fist. "If you come near me—or Clarissa," I shouted, "I'll give your fucking files to the cops." How weird, my voice was like the Dink's, kind of braying. "You creep, if anything happens to me— or Thelma or—" I didn't mention Eloise. "If you fuck over any animal, vegetable, or mineral...."

"Alton, you can be the master," he said softly and hiccupped. "I'll be the slave."

"No way!" I shouted. "Leave your Silver-Wraith parked on Red Square at midnight, as a token of good faith." I don't know why I had to echo his words. At least I didn't say "in point of fact."

I hung up and tore off the Dying Warrior. Shit, I'd forgotten to call him a prick.

☦

I got out my notebook. "Make something up, Alton," a scratchy voice said. I got out my *Yes, I Don't Love You* and copied the opening words in my notebook:

> Eloise Hartwig stared at the wreck of her VW Bug, Brunhilda.

As an experiment, I added one fact, writing:

> She went to the Bluestone Apartments because—

Because why? "Because Alton Broome needed her!" I shouted.

"No, you don't need me," said Eloise, far away. "You'll still have dreams, and—"

"Eloise!" I called out.

Nothing. I stared at the blank page. I wrote:

> "Come back."

Nothing. I pictured other things, a fantasy life for Eloise and me in the Vegetarian League, back in 1969. My life with

Clarissa hadn't happened. I read my words, "Come back."
They were just words.

"Emily, you made me up!" I shouted. "You can bring
her back." I didn't know if I meant Clarissa or Eloise. I ran
to the kitchen, opened a can of smoked oysters, gulped a
handful, opened another can. My marriage was over, and
so was my career. I let out a howl. My antique Kenmore
stove stared at me. I stared back, my mind a blank. I was a
reader, not a writer. I belched. I wasn't very creative.

I ran to the phone. Shit, I thought, I should call the man
from Emily's class who worked for Island Security. He said
he could get me a job. I'd have time between rounds to
write in my notebook. I'd help Emily. *Damn her and her damn
non-husband, too. My life's a mess. I'm broke. Emily's gone. Eloise
is gone. I should call my parents. Damn, writers are never here
when you need them.*

It was almost midnight when I dialed the number of the
New Whatcom. The clerk gave me my parents' room,
number two.

"Just a minute, I'll get your mother." That was Boomer,
putting her on the other extension, as per the usual. I didn't
know how they'd gotten a motel room with two extensions,
but I figured Emily was taking care of details.

"We've been worried—"

"You never write—"

"She told us—"

"Get help—"

The warm, familiar voices sounded like the two-headed
being in my dream. I was shaking.

"Mom, Dad, I'm all right. My marriage is over. I quit my
job. Or I was fired, I guess. But I'm starting this new life."
I stopped. I didn't have to tell them about my being in a
story yet. At least I hadn't woken them.

"Oh, Alton," said my mother, "when can we see you?"

"How about my place, lunch tomorrow?"

"Lunch? Is your stove working?"

"Lunch? What about—"

"We've come all this way—"

I don't know what came over me, but I heard myself say, "Mom, Dad, I'm glad you came. Just stop interrupting. And stop worrying. I'm okay."

The line went dead. Shit, I knew it. If I ever opened my mouth, my parents would never speak to me again. Maybe my father had heard me say I didn't use his shoetrees. Why couldn't Emily make things work out with them?

Fuming, I got a phone book, dialed Emily's student. "About that job you mentioned?"

A bit groggily, he said he'd already inquired. "Talk to...."

I jotted down the name of his boss and slammed down the phone, panting.

My couch was threadbare, my rug was frayed, and I missed my agates and geodes. So this was my real life. Maybe I could get my rocks from my office, what was left of them. I gritted my teeth.

It was after midnight when I parked the Valiant and snuck up the path over Sehome Hill through the arboretum behind campus. The dark, dripping fir trees swayed above me. I kept looking over my shoulder for Stevens.

At the back of Angel Hall, I pried open a loose manhole cover and climbed into one of the steam tunnels the cops had used back in the '60s to haul student demonstrators out of buildings. It was right where Emily had described it in *Yes, I Don't Love You.*

I felt my way in the clammy dark toward a light, a halfway-open door. I climbed echoing metal steps past the Chem labs, pausing in the dim hall by Stevens' office. It seemed odd I'd first read about Eloise here. I went to the roof and peered out over Red Square. There sat the Silver-Wraith, spray-painted, all by its lonesome, under a streetlamp on the wet, dark square.

I waited an hour, but no one came. Relieved, yet more than a bit edgy, I snuck down to my office, said hello to my rocks, the ones I had left, my geode with its cleft chin, my thundereggs, a hunk of obsidian. Damn Clarissa. I should've taken one of her jewels. That's what Eloise would've done. I turned out the light, lay down and curled up on the floor, closing my eyes. "Emily better send her damn non-husband back where he came from," I muttered.

The ventilators whirred. For a second, I thought I was back on the floor of good old number one. Or was it number two? I rolled over, between sleep and waking.

✝

Eloise and I were at my bank, not in number one, but in number two, where I'd never been before. We sat on the floor, side by side, naked. We hadn't gotten that damn B.C. Two glasses of Drambuie glowed by her feet. She hefted the obsidian. When I reached out, the rock fell and one of the glasses shattered. "I never even got my own fucking Cuisinart," she said sadly.

"Oh, Eloise," I murmured, putting my arm around her waist. We lay back. I scissored my leg between hers. I moved my head down and parted the lips of her vagina. She gasped. She tasted salty, a bit acidic, nice. She held my head in her hands. Small cries went up around me.

"Come in me, Alton. I want you in me."

When I did, it was hard to tell which sensation was in her, which was in me. Our sweaty bodies bumped and slapped together on the cold, gritty floor. I lasted a long time, as I did my last time with Clarissa. Eloise came, and then I came. She lay asleep beside me. I stroked her eyes, her eyebrows. She stirred. Her eyes came open. They were Emily's green-brown eyes, crinkled at the corners. As we sailed over the Grand Canyon, the Bright Angel Shale, Eloise held out a book to me.

✝

I woke up on the cold floor of my office, back aching. Where was Emily? If she could give me dreams, she could damn well give me the real thing. I stretched, got up. *I should clean my apartment. I should pack up my core samples.* My parents were coming. In a fit, I packed my best rocks in shoeboxes, ran down the hall to the utility closet and got a cart. As I heaped my boxes in, one spilled. Out came my geodes and thundereggs, and at the bottom of the box lay a rolled-up yellow page. I unrolled it. On a legal-size page was Eloise's lizard-like scrawl. The page ended with the words, "She held out a book." It was what I had just dreamed.

The sun came up as I wheeled my cart across the empty square. My rubber-soled Hush Puppies scuffed on the gravel of the parking lot near the overlook facing the bay and the Canadian Coastal Range. Kicking straight the small, black wheels, I heaved the cart out of a rut, hugging my shoeboxes, resting my chin on top of the pile.

I remembered how my father's shoetrees used to glare at me when I went to shine his shoes. I thought of one summer vacation when I was six and I carried my father's shoes and shoetrees to the Oldsmobile. Landy panted mournfully, sitting in the back seat on top of a mound of suitcases, water skis, and hatboxes.

"Mommy, are we moving?" I cried.

She sighed. "Boomer, I'm putting my foot down. He's got to sit somewhere."

"Not take my shoes, my shoetrees?" My father sounded injured.

"There's room here," I piped up from the back seat, perched atop a pile beside Landy.

I heard bits and pieces of their talk. The ability to listen to two people making reasonable suggestions at the same time was a talent I'd picked up early. Clinking his ring on the steering wheel, my father said something about not blocking the driver's view. My mother agreed about not blocking his view but said three pairs were unnecessary. Landy howled.

"It's settled," my mother said.

"No, it's not. Landy wants to take the shoetrees, doesn't she, Alton?"

"You contradict me, after I put my foot down?"

Landy bayed, my mother put her foot down, and my father mentioned the driver's view just one more time that I could tell.

"Let's just go," I said, and Landy and I made a comfy nest, three pairs of shoetrees lodged under us and three lying off to one side. We compromised, you could say.

✟

Now as I wheeled my cart across the parking lot, the sun came out over Sehome Hill, shining through the mist, a small, wan ghost. I felt good, the way I did that summer morning when I was six.

The fir trees on Sehome Hill uprose from the fog, shaggy as mastodons. The alders stood straight and tall, glinting as the sun shone through a narrow concourse in the cloud cover. I felt alone and excited, as if I were Adam or the first man to emerge from the mists that shrouded the planet for eons, as the rains came down and the planet cooled from the molten lump it had been after the solar system exploded.

I knew men hadn't walked out of those mists. After countless millenia, maybe a single-celled organism squiggled. But right now I was the man walking out of the mists. I heaved my cart forward, chugging away from my old life that vanished with the mists as I kept walking.

I put my head back and let out a howl the way Landy did when the mailman came. Giving my cart an encouraging hug, I looked around for the Valiant. Then I remembered I'd parked it on the other side of Sehome Hill. *Shit, shit.*

Cheer up, I told myself. *You're in a story.*

Over the bay, the mountains were cut sharply as the back of a stegosaurus, sculpted like a spine of blue ice.

"Unreal," I shouted. "What figments!" They looked fictional. I never felt better in my life.

✢

With my shoeboxes heaped high in the back seat, Eloise's page tucked in my wallet, I headed for the Miracle Laundromat. Wheeling my cart up the gravel path through the arboretum had been no laughing matter. I'd have a little chat with Emily.

I screeched the Valiant to a halt. A sign on the door of the Miracle said *CLOSED FOR REPAIRS*. I let out a howl. I rattled the doors. "Eloise, let me in!" I don't know why I thought she was there. I pounded on the glass door. It shattered. I stepped back, gasping. My hand was bleeding. I put it to my lips and licked it. For a second, I thought I was back at the lake. Or was it cubicle number two, in my dream? I thought of what Thelma had said about Emily looking for me, about her writing. And about the vault.

"Yippety-yi-yay!" I shouted, backing the Valiant out onto Holly Street, just missing a milk truck. My old clunker wouldn't do more than twenty in reverse, but I didn't care. I garnered strange looks, but no cops came. So far, so good. 8:10 a.m., the banks weren't open. *Damn bankers, they take your money, and they never do anything. Eloise is right.* I got out of the Valiant, sat down in the doorway of the Moose Lodge, and took off my shoes, as she once did. Closing my eyes, I dozed. My head jerked up. It was after nine. I put my shoes on.

✢

"Let me in—cubicle number two!" I yelled at Mr. Vault as I clung to his steel-barred door, glancing nervously at the walls of gray and silver boxes, scared Clarissa would pop out any second, her hospital eyes offering bribes.

Mr. Vault sighed, shook his head, licked his bulldog lips. "You don't want to fondle the valuables?" He frowned. "How about some words from the faithful Moody?"

"Number two, number two," I insisted, and scrawled a big *A* across his book.

He clanked me in, and I ran to cubicle number two, though its red "occupied" light was on. Pulling my collar up so I'd look tough, I jerked open the door.

A woman wearing jeans and a black turtleneck sat by a white counter under the recessed ceiling light. One shoe and sock were off, and with a bandaged hand she picked at her toenails. On her good wrist, she wore a plastic hospital I.D. bracelet. She looked up.

"Alton, you snoop." Emily Weed stood up, her face red. Gathering her yellow legal pad, she held it to her breasts.

I shivered. "Me a snoop? You are. You read my notebook." My throat was hot and dry.

"I didn't read your damn notebook."

"And you're moving without even telling me? And, and—you've been with *him*." I snarled my James Cagney snarl.

"Well, what of it, Alton? Where've *you* been?" She nervously brushed back an imaginary strand of hair from her forehead as she did long ago. "What do you want? To be in a story?" She tapped her foot. She was trying to sound matter-of-fact. She didn't seem to know I *was* in a story. I beamed, trying to help her remember.

Her dark-ringed eyes shone, bright and tired. "And what are you grinning about, Alton?"

I blushed and held out my cut hand, but she looked at me, uncomprehending. I thought of how I left her at the lake. I lowered my hand.

"At the lake—" I paused. Emily didn't seem to remember she'd been kidnapped.

She shot me a suspicious look. "Who told you I'm moving there, huh? And who told you I'd be here?" She slapped her forehead. "Oh, Thelma, right, I knew that. I'll kill her. Shit, shit."

"I had this dream, Emily—"

"This is the real world, Alton." Her voice was cold. For a second, she looked scared. Probably writing in her head again, just like Eloise said. *Why doesn't she remember, dammit?* And then I thought, *If she remembers, she'll know I left her.*

"You saw your non-husband, didn't you, Emily?" I demanded. If he or that damnable Dink laid a hand on her, I'd punch his lights out.

Emily's eyes widened. She tried on a laugh. "Yeah, the jerk. We got really stoned, and it was bad stuff, and I ended up in the hospital one night. I still get flashbacks. I've got to work. I can't finish. Oh, why am I telling you this?" She threw down her pages on the counter, held her bandaged hand with the other hand.

"What did you do to yourself, Emily?"

"I punched out his car window." She laughed. "It didn't break."

"I'm sorry," I said. I meant, sorry his window didn't break, sorry she didn't remember breaking my car window. *I'm a shadow,* I thought. *I'll disappear any second.* For a second, I glimpsed her—Eloise—the way she was before she first left me at the Counseling Center, telling me she wasn't the sort of person who fades into the woodwork.

Now Emily was playing with the door handle of cubicle number two, as Clarissa once did. I had to tell Emily. Eloise had always been direct with me.

"I'm a shadow, Emily," I said.

She laughed. "What do you mean?"

"If you don't know...." My voice trailed off. "I'm in your book." I reached out my hand. Emily stepped back, eyes wide.

It was cold in number two, and the ventilator whirred. Clarissa was right. The vault was weird. I started to cry. "Oh, Emily, I've tried so hard." Hadn't Eloise said that? "And, and...." I ached to say something else. I never should've left Emily at the lake.

Her voice rose. "So I wrote a few pages about you licking your damn window, Alton. What's the big deal? And how did you know about that?" She pursed her lips, stared at me accusingly.

A scared look came across Emily's face. She sucked in her breath. She was gazing past me, eyes rapt and tired. *Oh, no, she's somewhere else. I'll melt right here, in number two, our first time here together. My own parents don't treat me as if I'm real. They just hang up on me.*

As if through layers of water, I heard Mr. Vault's door clank open. The facing page on Emily's legal pad was blank. A few other pages had been rolled over. "You've been writing about us, haven't you, Emily?" I sounded accusing, though I had no right to accuse her.

Emily trembled, all but swayed. "I've been writing about *her*."

Did she mean Eloise or Meg?

"Shit, my sister left me, Alton. Oh, what am I saying? I made her leave. She took drugs. She took everything. She took my boyfriends. But I fixed her. I stole her birth control pills. Ha, so there. It's out. But she didn't get pregnant. She left, and then she died." Emily held her forehead, sobbing.

The white walls went blurry. Emily grasped my hand, and I squeezed it tight. "I lost half my pages, Alton, that night we threw things out. Serves me right. I can't finish my book—my books—and—" She was crying. "And I love you, Alton." She threw herself into my arms.

"Emily, I love you."

"No, you don't. Don't say that."

She huddled against me, her breasts and hips warm and real. A shadow, a man in a story, I held her. Emily had said relationships with fictional characters have drawbacks. Relationships, plural; characters, plural. But she never said marriage to one fictional character has drawbacks.

"Will you marry me, Emily?" I asked in a low voice.

She drew back, laughing a strange, half-pleased, half-angry laugh. "No, I *won't* marry you. There, are you relieved?"

"I don't think so."

"You don't *think* so?" She shook her head. "You don't want a real woman, Alton."

There it was. I shivered, but I didn't disappear. "Emily, I talked with my wife. About a divorce." I drew her to me, but she pulled back.

"I feel...so shattered, Alton. If I could just finish—" Eyes wild, Emily looked at me hopefully, as if I were that ending.

All right, the story's not over. I haven't split. Emily can give me a reunion with my parents, a quickie divorce, my teaching job back, with tenure. Shit, I forgot to ask Stevens that. The shadows in the walls of number two were stuccoed like the ones in my parents' basement.

"I have your pages, Emily."

"You do?" She gasped, frowned.

I hated Emily's frown. Eloise didn't frown like that. I frowned, too. "Stories can change things," I said, trying to warn her.

She touched my cheek and smiled a gorgeous smile. I felt, I don't know, so honored. We kissed—a big, wet kiss.

There was a knock on the door.

FIFTEEN

My father and mother stood in the doorway, Thelma
off to one side. Gazing up shyly with his intent, dark
eyes, Boomer Broome smiled as if to reassure me about the
extinction of the dinosaurs. He carried his old black
briefcase under one arm, and he looked oddly small. So
did my mother, who frowned, peering at me wet-eyed, as
if from far away. Had my dog Landy just died? Maybe we
all died sixteen years ago when I came out here.

"What is this, Grand Central Station?" wailed Emily. "I
just want a quiet place to write."

"Are we interrupting?" asked my father, shuffling his
feet, glancing from Emily to me. He was talking so softly,
as if he thought I was made of glass.

Emily laughed. Her hair was mussed, and one tail of
her blouse had pulled out. She tucked it in. I took a deep
breath. My father turned as if to leave.

"We didn't even—" My mother sighed. At her feet was
a large box that said *Amalgamated Rotisserie and Toaster Oven*.
So she was going to Do Something about my stove.
Frowning, she took my father's arm.

"Mom, Dad, I'm getting a divorce." I didn't have to be
reasonable; I was in a story. I smiled at Emily, and she smiled.

"Oh, Alton." My mother sounded as if I'd broken her favorite piece of china.

"Claire, Claire." My father shook his head.

"Well, I'm his mother. I've got an interest. And, he hung up on us."

"I didn't hang up," I said hotly.

"Neither did we," said my father, in a low voice.

"Well, you don't have an interest. You're my parents." I turned to my father. "I'm not shining your shoes anymore. And—and I don't use shoetrees. And I don't use rotisserie ovens."

My mother gasped, my father's head revolved toward hers, and my mother's turned toward his. For a second, they were two-headed, as in my dream at the lake. I hoped my mother wouldn't bring up the subject of a wedding, that "perglomination" Eloise had dreaded. This was neither the time nor the place.

"Mom, Dad—" I broke off, crying. Amazing, they weren't talking at the same time. "I love you both."

My mother sighed. "We love you, too, dear."

Smiling a dark, pleased smile, my father changed the subject. "I've got something for you, Champ," he muttered gruffly, pulling out a stack of yellow, legal-sized pages from his briefcase. Emily glanced down, mouth open. "A woman at the airport, she said these were for you. Drove right up on the sidewalk, almost hit us."

My father shook his head and looked at Thelma as if for further facts, but she only smiled her melancholy smile.

I inspected the pages. The handwriting wasn't Emily's— it was Eloise's scrawl, the same as in her postcard care of the Miracle. I grinned at Emily. She looked puzzled.

My mother's left eyebrow went up. "The young lady said it was up to you, Alton. And then she drove off just like that in one of those hippie cars. In *reverse*."

My father glowered. "Claire, her exact words were: 'Tell Alton. It's up to him.'"

"That's what I said, Boomer. It was up to him."

Emily smiled. "How did this mystery woman know what plane you'd be on, I wonder?" she asked my mother.

Claire turned to Thelma. "But you called us, dear."

Thelma laughed. "No, I didn't."

I remembered Eloise tapping her foot when my parents called me at the Bluestone. "The woman who called, did she have a real scratchy voice?" I asked.

"Facts are facts," said Boomer, nodding.

I squared my shoulders. Mr. Vault's steel door with its locks and clocks and wheels gleamed. It was as if my life lay stacked in deposit boxes, real as the rock layers of Washington: Okanagen Subcontinent, Kootenay Arc, Nooksack Formation. Having split off from Pangaea, these suspect terrains had docked in me. Funny, I didn't feel like a shadow now.

I hugged my father and mother. I hugged Emily.

"Are we going to be in your book, too?" asked my father, peering intently at Emily, who laughed a strange laugh.

"I write fiction," she said, clipping her words precisely.

I grinned and took her hand.

‡

"Okay, let's see it—the real thing," said Emily, pursing her lips. Her voice had that edgy gaiety.

My parents safely back at the New Whatcom, I was grateful—awed Eloise had brought them back to me—but I couldn't face her pages. Or rather, Emily's seeing them, seeing me.

Afternoon sunlight shone through the Bluestone's dusty windows, brightening the hunk of obsidian on my bureau. Emily and I sat on my green sofa. In the kitchen, Eloise's pages lay nestled in my father's briefcase. Past the glass doors, his shoetrees glowered in the closet. Wooden effigies of imaginary feet, each with a black, metal hinge, they rested on the floor beside my Hush Puppies, regarding me like fallen idols.

I dug out Miss Bosom's packet from my closet, my so-called earthly effects. I showed Emily her description of my licking the window.

She laughed, embarrassed. "Old business, Alton." Her dark eyes were intent, as when she stared at me in class long ago. I'd been the teacher then. Now, out the window, the blue outline of Lummi Island glowed, shadowy across the bright water.

I fetched back her drafts I'd rescued, along with the bits and pieces about her sister. Maybe that was the book we were in. Emily rifled pages, sighed as if in relief, lingered over a paragraph about how she and Meg grew up, making up fairytales about two wise, stubborn goats.

Eyes intent, Emily said hungrily, "Let's see it all."

Her leg brushed mine. I got up, brought over my father's briefcase, and sat back down. *Oh, no, when Emily reads this, she'll send me back to Clarissa, make me lick windows till my tongue freezes, probably make me shine my father's shoes, too.*

Slowly drawing out the legal pages, I thought of my dream of Eloise in number two. I blushed.

Emily rested one hand on my hand. "I can't make out the writing. You read it, Alton."

My heart pounded as I loudly read Eloise's scrawl: "'Once upon a time I was a reasonable man. That was before the divorce, before the trial separations, and before I fell in love with a fictional character, a woman in a book of short stories.'"

I groaned. It was my story. He was me. I was in her story. In spite of her dyslexia, Eloise had copied what Emily wrote. A wave of love and gratitude washed over me.

"It's all here," I cried.

"He sounds like you, Alton. Dry, modest, ardent." Emily's lips trembled. "*She* wrote this?"

I ran to my closet, tossed the Dying Warrior to one side, and snatched Eloise's postcard from the Miracle. If Emily sent me to float over the islands forever, so be it.

Shaking, I handed Emily the card. She turned it over, held it up next to one of the pages, and let out a laugh, not Eloise's laugh, not so much of a chortle, but nice. "Maybe we're in *her* book, Alton."

I thought of my first dream of Eloise waving a novel—her novel—outside Lincoln Center. I groaned. Then I grinned. If Emily and I were in Eloise's book, I wasn't alone. I sat down, glowing.

Emily was rereading what I'd read, tracing lines with one finger, moving her lips. Funny, now she could make out what I'd read aloud. She nudged me with one arm. "That's not bad. 'Once upon a time' is a bit cute. It should be 'Once I was a reasonable man.' And she shouldn't mention the divorce. That gives it all away." Emily fished out a red pen from her purse, made the correction, threw down the pen. "You're not going back to her, are you?"

"No." Did she mean Clarissa or Eloise?

She sighed, snuggled closer. "Keep going, Alton."

My chest ached. I read on, reliving my life with Clarissa, my rapture with Eloise, and my return. It was painful, embarrassing—more than embarrassing—my whole dumb life right there on the page. How could Emily have given me such a life? More than once she laughed, of all things. Or, half-astonished, half-scared, she glanced sideways at me, as if trying to remember something.

I read on haltingly, often stopping to ask if she were following me—following her copyist, Eloise, I meant. I didn't know why Emily didn't remember, but I breathed easier as I saw her crooked smile, her eyes bright. She didn't hate me. Maybe she needed me, her faithful reader. I'd be her interpreter, her typist, so long as she didn't uncreate me.

When I couldn't read Eloise's scrawl, sometimes I added a word, and I still didn't disappear. Late in the afternoon, the islands held the light, blue-white and milky. The last words I read were Emily's, just before I left her at the lake: "You could've had a real woman, not a story."

Emily took the page and set it down on the couch. She sighed. Her leg brushed mine. "What *do* you want, Alton?" Her dark-edged eyes shone. She was beautiful, painfully beautiful.

I put my arm around her thin shoulders, and the pages spilled to the floor. We kissed. She pressed her lips to mine in a sober, urgent way. I drew back, picturing Eloise, her gold eyes. I'd felt more—what?—real with her.

"What's the matter, Alton?"

I winced and got up, Emily following. She squeezed my hand, laughed. Damn, I still have any B.C.

Somehow we were walking, Emily and I, through the glass doors. My bed was unmade, the bedroom dim, my curtains drawn. I could see us saying goodbye when she wrote, "The End."

"Lie down, Alton," she said, mimicking Eloise's scratchy voice.

I shivered. My throat was tight. We were living what we'd read. Maybe I should get us two glasses of Drambuie the way Eloise did.

Emily gave me a little smile. We kissed. We were undressing. Emily's shoulders were thin. I held her gingerly as we sat on the bed. Her breasts were pale. Two dark hairs curled from her right breast. It seemed wrong to look.

"Maybe I should go put in my diaphragm," she said softly, and she got up and went away. Next to the Dying Warrior in my closet, my father's shoetrees glared.

She came back. She was kissing me. Her hands were cool. We lay down. She put her tongue in my mouth. I drew back.

"What's the matter, Alton?"

"Um, I don't know."

She sighed, stopped. We both knew what was the matter. I wasn't hard.

I sat up, hung my head. Looking up, I glared at her. *Damn this story. Damn Emily, too. Now she'll really write me off, snick-snack.*

She stood up, clutching her clothes to her breasts. "You never wanted me!" she cried. "You want *her*."

The scar on Emily's neck showed red in the light through my gauzy curtains. I swallowed hard.

Her voice rose. "I took your damn Intro course *two* times, and you didn't remember me. I hate geology. I hate writing. It gave me wrinkles. It made me sick. I don't exist for you. No wonder your wife—" She caught her hand to her mouth. She wept.

I went to her. Why didn't Emily understand I was in her story?

She swept my obsidian off the bureau. It fell and clattered on top of Eloise's pages. "You're just like *her*, Alton," Emily said, almost shouting.

My mouth dropped open.

"Not Eloise. Meg! She left, and then she died. Like my father. He's never there. Like my non-husband." She held one hand to her forehead, sobbing. "And you'll leave me, too. You don't love me."

Emily stood there, her face red and blotchy. She was thin, frail, almost swaying, arms crossed over her breasts.

I heard a scratchy voice in my head say, "Do something, Alton." I reached out and rested my hands on Emily's cool shoulders. She trembled.

"I could try—" I meant, try to be more real. "It's hard being a shadow in your book, Emily."

"*My* book?" She caught her breath.

"Well, aren't I?" I demanded.

"No," she shouted. "You're not unreal."

Emily touched her hand to my cheek. "*I* live with shadows, Alton," she said sadly, giving me an aching look. "I'll never have a real life. They'll never hire me full time. I'll never get married. Never write a novel. Just stories.

Never have a major credit card." She stuck out her chin, bravely. "I'm a fake. You'll find me out. I'm not a real writer. I wrote all these extraneous pages, and then I stopped. My editor says I lost my nerve." She glared. "I was writing two books, Alton—one about my sister and one about...." She frowned. I frowned.

"I couldn't finish. And I can't sleep. I've got these unpaid parking tickets. I eat meat. And I went to the vault one time, and I heard you. So I thought—" Emily blushed; I blushed. "I thought maybe if I went there to write—" She smiled her crooked smile.

So Emily liked the vault, too.

"Alton, when you told me you loved Eloise, I thought someday you'd see *me*." Her voice got soft. Her eyes were dark, soft. "Eloise is *me*. I kept waiting, ever since I met you at the folk dance, six months ago. Which you don't even remember."

Emily wept. I held her, kissed her forehead, her chin, her lips. I didn't care if her forehead was bony. If she'd just *told* me I was supposed to see Eloise in her, I'd have seen it. At our feet, Eloise's pages lay all interbedded.

"Emily, before I met you—" I meant before she made me up.

She pressed herself against me. "There, does that feel real, Alton?"

I breathed in and held her tight. Her eyes, green-brown, had light flecks at their edges, like, like....

I drew her to me, kissed the scar on her neck, bent down, nestled my face in her belly. If I couldn't do the real thing, I could still... and if I couldn't do that, we could read together. She liked to read with me. Amazing, I was getting hard. Her hands were in my hair, pulling me to my feet.

"Alton, let's lie down," she whispered.

Holding hands, we walked to my bed, lay down, kissed.

"Will you hold me—hold me and rock me?" she said. "It's been a long time."

I held her; I stayed hard. We kissed and kissed.

"Do you want to come in me, Alton?" she asked softly.

I got on top. She was wet, her pubic hair scratchy, and she was tight. Trembling, I came almost at once.

"I'm sorry, Emily," I said.

"Don't say that." She squeezed my shoulders, kissed my face. I was subsiding. I came out of her with a soft pop, moved my hand down to her crotch, but she pushed it away.

"Just hold me, Alton."

I wanted to tell her I'd do better the second time. Tell her she'd finish her book, her books. I had faith in her.

I lay still, and her breathing got low, but she wasn't asleep.

"Will you tell me a story?" I asked softly.

She smiled, opening her eyes, and a pained, rapt look crossed her face.

"What went wrong with you and your sister, Emily?" I asked, holding her tight.

"If I could just see her one last time." Emily nestled closer. Her cheeks were wet. "You know, when we were kids, my dad used to drive us by the mustard fields in Skagit Valley. Near Padilla Bay, sometimes we'd see these flocks of little birds. Dunlins, you know? They keep flashing in and out of the light. Disappearing, then coming back. White, black, white! Like they're flashing in and out of this life and some second life. Over all that gray water.... Oh, Alton, if I could just tell her I love her and I forgive her for dying, and she doesn't have to worry about me anymore, then maybe...."

She wiped her eyes in her precise way, first one hand, then the other.

"What went wrong with you and your sister?"

"Alton, before she left, she'd been a street person. Sleeping in her car, taking drugs. She didn't have anywhere to go, and I didn't stop her, and—" She buried her face in my neck. "Oh, Alton, I'm scared to write about her, scared to go back to the lake."

Emily was sobbing. I rocked her and kissed her eyes, stroked them softly. I held her, and she pressed herself against me. We kissed. I was hard. She put her hand on my penis, stroked the length of it lightly. I parted the folds of her vagina. She was wet.

"Maybe I should get on top, Alton." Her voice was scratchy, low.

She knelt on top of me, put me in her, leaned back slowly. I gasped. I opened my eyes. She was big, up there above me. I was deep inside her. I drew her down to me. We kissed, moved together. Her body tightened, clasped. Her cries went up. My cries got closer to hers. I came with a yell. She strained against me, stopped.

"That was fun," she said, out of breath.

"You didn't come, did you?" I asked sadly.

"Don't ask me that."

We came apart. The islands were blue-dark, and she nestled closer. I hugged her. I wanted to ask her if she'd still read with me, but I couldn't ask her that. And then the words came out.

"Will you still read with me, Emily?"

"You want to *read* with me, Alton?" Her laugh rose to a wail. "Oh, you *do* love me." She kissed my forehead, and soon her breathing got low.

✝

I raised myself on one elbow. The islands were silhouettes, blue-black at the edges. Borne a few centimeters a year on the conveyor belt of the Pacific Plate, they had made their journey across the ocean. Scoured by glaciers, rounded by those recent abrasions, they rose up, almost imaginary.

For a second, I wasn't sure where "here" was. In my closet, the Warrior lay cuddled up with my father's shoetrees.

For a second, I saw myself back in New York in the Sixties, taking a seminar in a tall building with a helmet of black plexiglass on the top floor. Standing in the light, Stevens asked me to read seminar topics aloud—rifted margins, forearc basins, ancient collisions.

He called the proponents of continental drift "the Drifters," said the stake hadn't been driven into the vampire's heart and Wegener's old theory was back. Stevens laughed at the geophysicists who called the earth a self-exciting dynamo.

Back then the paleomagicians dragging magnetometers from ships hadn't yet turned up the Mid-Atlantic Ridge, spreading a few centimeters a year, and no one guessed what might move the magic carpet until the seismology boys came through. Watching their jiggling needles, they read how a layer of molten rock sixty miles down rafts the continents over the earth. Fueled by the heat of convection, they spin like cream in your morning coffee.

"Continental drift," Stevens had said disgustedly. "Plates of the lithisphere can't float over the globe like so many *Kon Tikis*!"

✟

Now Emily murmured something in her sleep, and I saw many things, as if we were reading, or as if I'd gone into her dream.

We were having dinners at the lake, two or three times a week. We were planting a garden, harvesting potatoes that cross-pollinated with tomatoes. At Emily's table, I was loath to touch things, for fear they'd come apart in my hands. Over and over, I asked Emily to marry me, but she said no. When I asked if she was the woman on Holly Street in the oriental jacket, she said no.

I was signing up for Emily's non-fiction writing course, but she changed the number on my permission slip to the number for fiction, her red pen big as a hockey stick.

I was standing on the big cedar stump at Boulevard Park by the bay. It was the day my divorce was to come through. Clarissa and I had had a fight in the courtroom. She said I should get the living-room carpet and she should get the house. I ran out of the courtroom and called Emily.

"If you won't tell me which book I'm in," I yelled, "I'm calling your editor in New York."

"Go ahead."

✝

"I'm in Emily's book," I told the editor. "I started out real, and then I was unreal, and now I'm real, Emily tells me. I wish she'd make up her mind."

"Hey, are you Alton? She told me about this nutty geologist she's been in love with two years."

"Two years?" He didn't have his facts straight. And what did he mean, nutty? "Yeah, I'm her narrator," I said.

He laughed. "That can't be."

I hated people laughing at me. Hmm, maybe Emily was writing non-fiction. How come everyone but me knew it? But this editor was in New York. It was his job to know things. Maybe I was real. No, that was too incredible.

✝

I drove downtown, poked my nose in Employment Security, and called out Eloise's name. I got my white-gold ring back from the pawnshop and then paused by the vault. Damn, why was this all happening? Our non-wedding—Emily's and mine—was coming up. My parents were flying out.

I stopped by a display window outside the Bon Marche. Behind a blond mannequin wearing red knickers hung a picture—Meg's drawing of the three women, 'AP' for artist's proof—and the crow wasn't on Eloise's shoulder.

I ran into the Bon. "Eloise, Eloise."

Carrying a rackful of bridal clothes, she ducked into the women's dressing room.

I barged in and tore open a curtain. Empty. I ripped the next curtain off its rod. Another, another.

A gray-haired woman wearing a slip yelled, "Get out of here, you creep! Someone call the cops."

I backed away. "Oops, sorry." Shit, if Emily was writing this, it wasn't funny.

I ran down aisles, bouncing off people like bumper cars and knocking over a display of women's underwear. A scratchy voice came from a mannequin wearing hiking boots, alpine shorts, and a big, dumb smile.

"Alton, it's me. Yoo-hoo!" It was the big E.

"I thought you wanted to go back," I said.

"It's so much fun driving the Porsche. I took it, by the way. You can have Brunhilda. I think your getting married again is neat. I always wondered what it's like, you know? I'm heading down to Mazatlan. Lie down by a warm brown sea." Eloise sighed. "By the way, I'm taking my novel. Our novel. Gotta split now."

"I'm coming with you!" I cried.

Fluorescent lights flickered. A security guard ran toward me. Shit, I knew him. He worked at Island Security, too. I raced out of the store, revved the Valiant in reverse, drove to a phone booth on Railroad Avenue across from Dow Jewelers, and I called Emily.

"How about if I wear hiking shorts at our non-wedding?" I asked.

Emily laughed. "Make it a real wedding, Alton."

"All right!" I shouted, grinning.

"All right."

✝

I was back in my bed at the Bluestone, murmuring, "All right, all right." Emily lay asleep, the sheet drawn to her neck.

In the twilight, islands and more islands—Eliza, Lummi,

Orcas—rose out of the water. Light from the living room shone through the glass doors on my faded carpet, on Emily's clothes, my clothes, my hunk of obsidian, my wallet with its ragged edge of yellow paper sticking out—Eloise's gift. But her pages were gone.

As I got up, a truck backfired. I ran to my window. A fourteen-wheel semi was towing a brown house on a big platform, turning off Holly Street onto my block. The windows in the house had been knocked out. It was Emily's house from Enterprise Road, halfway to its destination at the lake.

As I leaned out my window, the semi edged closer. There was a crash, broken glass, a screech of metal grinding. Two floor joists from Emily's house bashed through my Valiant's remaining side window and, like a forklift, raised my faithful car into the air.

In the cab of the semi, a woman wearing a red headband waved, squinting.

"Guess I do need glasses, Alton," she called out in her scratchy voice.

My chest ached. I felt—I don't know—awful and grateful.

The semi veered onto my lawn. There was a second crash like an after-shock, and the Bluestone swayed. Emily sat up in bed, let out a cry. The Valiant's hood rammed through my living-room wall, as if heaved up by the Pacific Plate in some new tectonic event. Broken glass littered the carpet. Plaster was falling. Wires dangled.

Emily bolted up. "Alton, isn't that your poor car? And what's that—on the hood?" She laughed, pointing.

Draped around the Valiant's hood ornament was what looked like a torn sleeve of the blue satin oriental jacket.

I grinned. A siren blared. Pulling Emily to me, I drew her through the wreckage to my bedroom window. The cab of the semi was driverless. A police car turned the corner as a man who looked like Stevens ran down the street. The police car pulled over, lights churning.

I put my arm around Emily's waist. "Is this…?" I paused. Didn't say, "The End." Didn't ask if my strange life with its sadness, joy, and mirth would no longer be fictional.

Emily leaned against me, the Bluestone shifted, and the shorelights from here to Gooseberry Point went out.

"Hi, Alton." She held my face in her hands.

Richard Widerkehr was born in New York City and received his B.A. from the University of Michigan, where he won two Hopwood Awards for Poetry. He received his M.A. from Columbia University. His poems and stories have apeared in numerous literary magazines, and have won prizes from the Pacific Northwest Writers Conference and the Leslie Hunt Award from Western Washington University. His poetry collection, *Disappearances*, was published by Radiolarian press.

Richard has lived in Bellingham, Washington, since 1978, working as a teacher in the Upward Bound Program and as a counselor and case manager at mental health clinics.

Tarragon Books

Tarragon Books is supported by grants from generous patrons of the arts. Our goal is to bring the work of Pacific Northwest novelists to readers everywhere who enjoy lively stories and distinctive voices. This is "fusion fiction," challenging the boundaries of genre and delineations of reality, striving to be both entertaining and thought-provoking.

Tarragon is the Dragon-herb, our logo adapted from a Viking carving of the winged serpent embodying wisdom and power.

‡

Also from Tarragon Books:

Islands by Sara Stamey. ISBN 0-9724986-1-3

A Northwest archeologist digs up a dangerous mystery while researching Caribbean petroglyphs.

"A superior mystery and suspense novel with solid characters, some very spooky goings-on, and lots of wonderful writing…An intellectual thriller? Absolutely. It's a fast read, a stomping, vivid ride, the work of a woman who is passionate about lots of things."
—Dan Hays, *Statesman Journal*